I0640859

Anonymous

Legends of Westmorland and the Lake District

Anonymous

Legends of Westmorland and the Lake District

ISBN/EAN: 9783337153922

Printed in Europe, USA, Canada, Australia, Japan

Cover: Foto ©Andreas Hilbeck / pixelio.de

More available books at **www.hansebooks.com**

John B. Tyson

A Birthday Gift from

his Affectionate Broth

William Tyson

31st October 1871

LEGENDS

OF

WESTMORLAND

AND THE

LAKE DISTRICT.

———————◆———————

LONDON:

HAMILTON, ADAMS, AND CO., 32, PATERNOSTER ROW.

KENDAL:

JAMES ROBINSON, FINKLE STREET.

1868.

GR
142
W5L52

CONTENTS.

	PAGE.
Sizergh Hall.—A.D., 1460 . .	3
The Anchorite's Well	22
The Castle Watch	31
Burneside Hall	38
Bernard Gilpin of Kentmere Hall .	68
The Stramongate Barghaist	111
The Raid of Prince Charles.—An Incident of 1745	123
Dunmail Raise	151
Leolf, the Avenger	173

SIZERGH HALL.—A.D., 1460.

"Hie thee home, Holliday, and tell Gertrude that her
brother's good sword has brought as noble an eagle
from his border eyrie as ever graced the hall of our
forefathers, whether as guest or prisoner."

The horseman addressed, immediately clapped spurs
to his steed, and then away went the boldest man at
arms whom the banks of bonnie Kent could shew, to
apprise the sister of Walter de Strickland, that her
brother was returning from a border foray with his
prisoners and spoil.

The party had just reached the height which commands a view of Kendal. The evening sun was hastening to its rest behind the magnificent Pikes; yet there
was abundant light to see the grey turrets of Burneside
Hall, the venerable-looking Hospital embosomed beneath overhanging woods, and the lordly towers of the
Castle of the Parrs; and Walter almost fancied he
could discern the loftiest peak of the Watchman's
tower, peering above the noble trees which encircled
Sizergh, the ancient mansion of his fathers.

Though young, Walter was no novice in border warfare; yet never had his previous success been so great
as at present. His eye turned to the group behind him,
as Holliday disappeared, but it was only for a moment.
His spirit was too lofty to add discomfort to the feelings
of the noble Greame, already chafed by his weary ride,
attended as he and the other prisoners with him had

A

been, by the young knight's retainers, and a select party
of Kendal bowmen.

The messenger had scarcely seen his faithful grey in
the stall, ere, by Gertrude's commands, the fires were
blazing on the open hearths of hall and kitchen, every
inmate of the fine old hall was in motion, and a repast
fit for the victors was speedily prepared—a repast becoming the age, and the hospitality of the Stricklands.

Gertrude had spent a solitary day at her tapestry,
the needle work of the period. She had been sketch-
ing passages from Roman history and the countenance
of Julius Cæsar was just receiving expression from the
artist's finger—the coloured wool was imparting life—
when the Porter's hall had resounded with the advent
of Holliday; and amid the bustle and stir of preparation the maiden's thoughts were turned to matters of
sterner import.

Gertrude was just ripening into womanhood; but
love had not yet fixed his shrine in her breast; though
never were kindred more devoutly loved than were
those of the female hope of the house of Strickland.
The library was her delight. An uncle's travels abroad
had enriched its shelves with the chivalrous literature
of Italy and of Spain. While the Provençal lays of
heroism and of love, had been added by another relative
who had followed Henry V. to the plains of France.
Here would Gertrude linger for hours, and when busy
at her needle, often would her intelligent eye seem to
be entranced in meditation on the richly illuminated
volumes she had been reading.

The long, resounding blast of her brother's bugle
had been heard through the low park, giving note of
his approach. It was twilight, but Gertrude had seen
him ascending the steps that led to the great hall, accompanied by a stranger of manly mien and bearing.

"Had your clan rescued you ere you reached my roof, sir," said Walter, "I should have had to answer to the Warden of the Marshes for the escape of so noble a prize; but now my walls are too strong, and the neighbouring moors too wild, for a solitary prisoner to escape. The Greame, therefore, may feel at home in the hall of the Stricklands."

"In troth, Walter," replied the captive, "you are too generous. If you wish me to pledge my word, I become a prisoner of honor and will not escape; but, if you hold your bolts and bars so firm as to require no gage, remember that the Greame of Lamplugh bears on his scutcheon, the mole, the fish and the eagle."

"I had not forgotten it," said Walter, "and if you can undermine my good walls, there are still too many rivers for a fish to swim, too many mountains for your eagle to overtop, and too many shafts from our bowmen to pierce his wing, between Helston and Eden. You may seek to revisit the boundaries of Ennerdale; may have the start of the stabled deer;—but ye should still revisit our old church of the Holy Trinity, ere the abbey of the Holme met your eyes."

"By my faith you are right, Walter," cried the gallant Greame, "if your hall be stored with bird-lime such as I see before me. An' that were the case, the most home-sick eagle would hardly flee away."

Strickland turned and saw his sister retiring from the presence of the stranger.

"Ah, Gertrude," he said, "I am a recreant to your kind care; but, believe me, it was the inspiration of a sister's love, and the angel of the fair flower of Conishead, that nerved my arm in the fray."

"No excuse now, Walter," said the maiden, "but hasten to your repast. A brother's love will ever repay my fondest care. But you shame your hospitality,

brother,—pray what companion in arms am I to welcome to our roof."

"'Tis Bertram Greame, of Lamplugh," answered
Walter, "whom the chance of war has given me for a
guest. I need not tell you that I wish every one here
to regard himself at home. Such has been, and I trust
will ever be, the feeling that welcomes the guests who
pass the threshold of Sizergh Hall."

"True," replied Gertrude, "but it may be that the
home of our gallant visitor is elsewhere, and his heart
there also."

" Even a prisoner, fair lady," said the Greame, "were
joyous, were you the light of his lonely dwelling."

The repast was ended, the hounds ceased to gambol
their glad welcomes around their master, and were
dreaming on the rush-covered floor, — the fire had
dwindled to embers, and all was still, save the footsteps
of the warder on the small area of the tower, telling of
the watchfulness that gave repose to the other inmates
of the ancient hall. Greame, though during the evening he enjoyed the courtesies of a guest, was conducted
at night-fall to an apartment in the tower, high from
the ground, and heard the bolts of a massive lock turn
on the oaken door, while Holliday's bed was laid in the
passage leading to the strong chamber: it mattered
little to Will, indeed, whether his couch was heather,
the rock, an oaken floor, or a straw pallet.

Greame slept not. Though fatigued, his eyelids were
not heavy. Did he meditate on his captivity,—brood
over the shame of his defeat,—or was he contriving his
escape? Ah, no! other cares oppressed him. The couch
had but lightly felt his weight, sleep was hopeless and he
paced his room with perturbed footsteps. Care had
already added gloom to that open forehead, and the
clustering ringlets of raven hair which curled around

it, seemed like the heavy clouds that horizon a thun-
dery sky. There was rigidness in that Grecian face,
and the curl of his lip betokened decision; but his
noble and lofty figure had lost somewhat of its undaunted bearing, and his whole man bore evidence
of a heart little at ease. Wherefore was the gallant Greame thus disturbed ? Bertram had trod
the hall of the great, and his hand had been courted by the rich and powerful. Beauty had gazed
upon him with delight, but his heart had been in
his armour, his horses, and hounds; and the beam of
loveliness shone on him in vain. But this was so
no longer. The gentle form of Gertrude had been
graven on his affections, and with a devotion as
deep as sudden, his whole soul was absorbed in her
attractions. Little did that fair lady dream, while she
calmly rested in her inlaid chamber, that she had
created in her visitor's heart a love which was as agoniz-
ing as he held it to be hopeless. Bertram felt that a
foeman's love would be regarded as insult, and he
dreaded a captivity which by the necessities of frequent
intercourse should add fuel to the flame that burned
within him. Yet 'tis doubtful whether, as he descended
by invitation to the breakfast apartment, he would
have made his escape, even had the gate stood open
before him and no one to bar his egress. Plenty was
spread on that ample board, and the hearty welcome of
Walter and his sister would have set Bertram at ease,
had not his feelings been easeless.   *   *   *

Walter's horse was at the door, and he was mounting to tell Lord Clifford, then on a visit at Kendal
Castle, the result of the foray, by way of indemnity to
that gallant Baron, whose illness had prevented him
heading the victorious party. "Greame," cried Strickland, "you will find books and musical instruments,

—the library,—all the rooms are at your disposal. My
horses and hounds, perhaps, were fitter for a border
chieftain, but I cannot trust you with these at present."
Bertram, from the hall window, watched the young
knight as he galloped through the park, attended by
his retainers, and often wished and unwished his re-
lease from captivity. An hour of anxious thought
seemed a forenoon, and he now bethought him to
divert care by surveying the apartments of his prison-
house. He entered one room where were carved the ar-
morial bearings and quartering of the illustrious owners.
Pictures—master-pieces in their day—graced the walls,
—the chess-board and games of puzzles, the silken
hoods and silver bells of the falcons overspread the oaken
tables. He passed on to another chamber, of which the
door was partially open. The tomes, with their wooden
sides and hinged backs, some gorgeously gilded, and
others as rough as the unplaned ash had left them, told
him it was the library. He was entering, when the
tuning of an instrument caught his ear, and the soft,
sweet voice of a female accompanying a vielle, commenced one of those wild but plaintive airs which were
common among the troubadours. He crossed the
threshold, and found Gertrude evidently studying the
lay which he had heard.

" I am intruding," said he.

" Nay," returned the damsel, unconscious of the effect
wrought upon her hearer, " I was merely relieving an
hour of study by practising one of those sweet strains
with which Ronsard has added harmony to my poor
essays in music."

" And pray, fair lady," replied Bertram, " what may
have been the studies which call for such relaxation ?
Debarred from the pursuits of the field, I must, monk-
like, turn to those of the closet, and I shall be lost

amidst these ponderous treasures of lore unless you be
my guiding star to point out where true knowledge is
to be found."

We need not give the maiden's reply. Suffice it
that she found in Bertram one whom deeds of war and
the chase had not, as with her brother, and most others
of that period, wholly withdrawn from the stores of
learning just emerging from the contempt under which
they had so long and so generally been held. Simi-
larity of taste, whether they searched the historic page
of Gregory of Turenne, the poetry of Chaucer, of
Gower, or Taverner, or the biography of Raimond
d'Agile, made the morning pass delightfully, and on
hearing the well-known sound of her brother's clarion,
Gertrude started with surprise at his apparently speedy
return, and found to her dismay that there were duties
neglected and servants in disorder. It as little became the lady of that day, as of this, to leave the
course of a large household undirected or uncontrolled.

It comports not with our brief narrative to describe
the hours of our captive. He was surprised that no
tidings reached him of a ransom ; yet his days hung
not heavily upon him. Walter was much with his
hawks and hounds, and in his absence Bertram and
Gertrude were ever found in the library, which
had become more and more a place of delightful
resort to both. The evenings were spent around
the hearth, enlivened by reciting tales, in which
the maiden fancied that Bertram excelled, or in the festive entertainment of numerous visitors, to whom Sizergh
was always open ; when amid the enchantment of music, and the gaiety of the dance, Bertram still shone to
others as to Gertrude, like the cedar of the forest, noble,
unchanging, and beautiful.

Ere long, the slumbers of Gertrude were broken.

The form of the captive would flit before her; his praises would haunt her waking hours; and, before she became conscious of the state of her own feelings, she loved. An avowal of her passion followed Bertram's imploring assurances of devotion, and oaths of fidelity were interchanged by moonlight on the terrace fronting the venerable pile. Greame now longed for his ransom, in order that, as an unfettered chieftain, he might come and demand his bride.

* * * * *

'Twas twilight, dimness had veiled the hall where Bertram, reclining on a low seat, was meditating; Walter approached him, attended by Holliday, but they saw not the captive.

"Tell him," said Walter, "that the riches of the border will not purchase his freedom."

"But, sir," said Holliday, "the messenger wishes to know why he is detained contrary to all rules of war, when any amount of ransom is offered."

"Let him come after our lady's festival," said the knight, "when our heart may be softened. We love his company too well to part with him ere then."

He passed on, and Holliday withdrew.

What, thought the captive, can this mean?—it doubtless relates to me.

It did so, and ere morning Bertram had learned from the night warder, to whom, as a prisoner in the border, he had once shown kindness, that the Warden of the Marches had commanded that the Eagle of the North should be kept pinioned until another foray had been made on the border, as he greatly dreaded both the sword and the counsel of the Greame. Wrathful on hearing this, his whole soul was roused as from a sleep of delight. He cursed the supineness with which he had willingly continued a prisoner. For a moment he fancied that Gertrude's enchantment had been a lure to reconcile him to his durance. Why had he not tried to escape? Why not sent directions by one of his pages, whom he had spied lurking about the Court disguised as a Kendal bowman, for an invasion to liberate him? A moment's reflection, however, freed Gertrude from his suspicions, and persuaded him that her love was worth the loss of half his herds and retainers. The thought of that love also nerved him to make an effort at escape, in order to avert the perils threatened his clan in his absence. His eyes were now opened. He saw, what was before unobserved, that evident preparations were in progress for a serious incursion. Arms were being furnished. An old storehouse of chain mail was opened, and armour and heavy falchions were being cleaned from the rust which had gathered upon them since they were last worn by Crusaders under the walls of Acre.

"I must leave you, dearest Gertrude," said Bertram, "but soon, I trust, to return."

"Has Walter agreed for your ransom," asked the maiden.

"I fear there is no chance that he will do so as yet: but my own arm must pay the price."

"What?" exclaimed the affrighted girl.

"The coming tears of the fatherless and widow rise before me; and the cries of the spoiled and the spoiler are approaching on the gale," answered Bertram.

He told the fair listener what he had heard. "'Tis ignoble—dastardly!" she cried, "to rob the Eyrie when the Eagle is bound."

Her dissuasions were henceforth exchanged for encouragement; though her heart still fainted at the thought of separation, and at the direful risks which Bertram would run in his attempt to escape.

B

'Twas morning, the sun shone joyously, and had
dimmed with its light the beacon fires, which on the
preceding night were blazing on Arnside, Farlton, Hay-
fell, and Whinfell, to summon the hardy mountaineers
and dalesmen to the rendezvous. Messengers were
hurrying between the castle and the respective towers
and fortified peels in the vallies. Clifford had resolved
to accompany the incursion, though, on account of his
illness, Walter was to be the real leader of the foray.
He had summoned two hundred of the Kendal bowmen,
who, having been allotted by the wardsmen, might
now be seen in their yards, and before the Newbiggin
in the open street, stringing afresh their bows and ex-
amining their keenly-pointed arrows.

"Where is Lord Stanley, the Warden of the
Marches?" was the general cry.

Walter, surprised at receiving no instructions, was
anxiously awaiting letters from that nobleman. Every
retainer at Sizergh was hastening preparations for the
enterprise; Bertram too, was nerving himself to escape
at all hazards, when a personage was announced as unexpected as fortunate. With a sable cowl closely en-
veloping his visage, and supported by a tall staff, a
venerable figure advanced into the court of Sizergh
Hall. The keys of St. Peter were embroidered in
scarlet cloth on his black cloak, while the bottle, scrip,
and faded branch which he bore bespoke him a holy
Palmer. His beard indicated age, yet the brightness
of his eye seemed to tell of younger days. The serving
men clustered around him, and the maids peeped from
the grated windows. His business was with Walter,
who advanced to meet him.

"Greet you well, noble Knight," said the Palmer,
"the Lord Stanley has given me, as I passed his abode,

a letter which he required to be delivered into no other hands than those of the Strickland."

"The father of Stanley would have sent a speedier messenger in time of war," replied Walter, "but thanks to you, holy sir, nevertheless; you are weary and must go in for refreshment."

Gertrude soon provided for the entertainment of the Palmer, who, in return, gave her a narrative of the shrines he had visited and the sufferings he had undergone.

Walter having read the letter seemed chafed, and addressing his sister, said, "so Stanley leaves me and the Clifford to win the day without his help, an' it were that the border chieftains were like himself we might find the game as easy to run down as the conies of the rock, but with such mettle as they possess we needed all our forces."

Finding that the Palmer had no additional verbal directions, Walter hastened the preparations, as the force was to set out in the evening of the following day.

Bertram, who had been painfully anticipating a parting with Gertrude, now approached from a small stone-floored apartment, which was more especially devoted to his use, and attracted to the hall by a voice which he thought he recognised, he drew near to the Palmer, and unobserved by Gertrude, received from the wallet of the holy man a packet with a sign of strict secrecy.

A moment sufficed for the perusal of these dispatches and to bid the Palmer await his reply.

Never had the Greame matters of greater moment to decide—never were his spirits less attuned to composure. From his letters he learned that the court in London had heard of his capture, and (regardless of border honour which, save in pillage, was equal to that of the most chivalrous times) had purposed to send instructions

during Walter's absence to surrender him up for re-
moval to London, preparatory to his trial and probable
condemnation, on account of various acts considered
gallant in northern warfare.

The Palmer had been to Stanley, appearing to him
as a religious wanderer, in order to be entrusted with
a message, and so gain admission into Sizergh. He had
now, at Bertram's service, in Kendal, four horses, apparently those of merchants, laden with silk and cotton
for Carlisle, and for the safe passage of which it was
customary to procure a letter of protection from the
leaders of the districts through which the travellers'
road lay. This had been obtained, as of course, from
the bailiff of the castle. It was dark when those horses
entered Kendal, else a good judge, and there was many
a one there in that day, would have told that with all
their ungainly housings and appointments, the steeds
had mettle and muscle which would stand a hard chase.

Bertram's agitated feelings became calm, as he chose
his course, and with a cool determination he resolved
on the venture. This was soon communicated to the
Palmer, and Bertram and Gertrude were again alone.
We will not unveil the sacred privacy of that interview
from which she came forth with a beam of anxious care,
and he with one of gratified but thoughtful decision.

On departing the Palmer again met Walter, who,
learning that the holy man was about to spend some
hours at Preston Abbey, invited him to return and make
the Hall his abode for that night. This he accepted ;
but the monks of Preston never saw the Palmer that
day, unless, with the second sight of their founder
Cospatrick, they beheld him along with the merchants
in the hostel of the Wool Pack in Kendal.

The evening had closed in—the Palmer was relating
his wonderful tales in the great hall. Walter lis-

tened with delight to the history of the gallantry of
one of the Crusading Stricklands which the narrator
himself had heard in the monastery of St. Peter, in the
holy city. Servant after servant made excuses for their
presence, until at last the hearth had gradually accu-
mulated around it the whole population of Sizergh.

It had been a hard day of preparation—the morrow
was to be one of movement. The flagon had gone round
and round, and the Palmer had ever a ready toast at command; while Will Holliday's songs of the border, from
their native humour, made the roofs ring and the pennons on the walls wave with the loud laugh of the
listeners.

"Now one of your French songs, Gertrude," said
Walter, turning to where his sister usually sat.

"She has just retired to her room," said one of the
maidens.

"Greame, it is your turn then," added he, "cannot
you sing a lay out of one of those books which I have
seen you poring over as if you intended to carry its
contents with you to Lamplugh."

Greame hesitated not, but sang:—

"The Christian Knight has been captive ta'en
By the Moorish bands in the fields of Spain.
Wail, clarion, wail, in a mournful strain,
For the Knight of the Cross is by infidels slain.

Joy to thee, clarion, sound once more,
For the Knight has escaped from the infidel's power;
'Twas a maiden's hand that has opened his door,
And delivered her love from the sword of the Moor.

Wake thee up, clarion—peal thee with joy—
For the marriage feasting thy notes employ—
The Moorish maiden is Christian now,
And the priest with the cross has signed her brow.

The Knight he has married his Saracen bride;
Dovelike and fawnlike she stands by his side;
And the sword of war it is sheathed awhile,
And peace o'er the olives of Spain shall smile."

The voice was rich, and as the noble air floated through the hall the Palmer looked around, but the music had enchanted the group, and as Gertrude was again taking her seat in the circle, Bertram was solicited to repeat the song.   He declined, but immediately commenced :—

"I love my horse, my hawk, my hound,
I love o'er field and heath to bound,
I love the chase, by sun or star,
But my plighted love is dearer far.

The goblet rich with roses twined,
Its pleasures round my bosom bind—
I love the joys of generous wine,
But nought, my love, compared with thine.

Men love the sword and fearful fight—
Priests love their tithes—lords love their might—
All love their lives—but I should be
Happy, my love, to die for thee."

The Palmer looked not up; Gertrude's eyes were bent downwards, but a beam of animation played over her flushed cheeks; Bertram was composed; while Walter's thoughts had wandered with the song to the fair lady of Conishead.

　　*　　　*　　　*　　　*　　　*

How is it that neither warder nor bay-dog heard the footsteps that gently trod across the hall of Sizergh at two hours past midnight?   The carousing of the evening had made their slumber deathlike, and the Palmer and Bertram signalled Gertrude—aye, Gertrude, whose eyelids had not been closed,—that the hour of departure was at hand.

Have you ever, fair reader, left your home?   If so, you may know something of the feelings of one who was leaving the roof of her fathers.   But do you know the maiden feelings of her who is about to commit her happiness to another.   We cannot describe them ;—it was love, and love is stronger than death.

The Palmer's companion had the horses at the gate ; all mounted, Kendal was soon reached. The wax seal dangling from the letter of protection and passport opened their way as they slowly passed through the town, while a noble to each wardsman, wherewith to buy some sack in the chill of the morning, made their passage still easier.

Now on the road, Bertram grasped the hand of his lady love, and wiped away the tear which had fallen, as she cast a lingering look, towards each one of the familiar objects of her childhood, while the whole flitted by and faded away in rapid succession.

"No time now for sorrow," said the Palmer. Every spur was struck deep, and fast over mountain and moorland did the party speed on their way. They crossed themselves as they passed the Druids' temple at Shap. Cautiously they hied between Penrith and Brougham castles, nor waited till in the thickets of Inglewood forest they halted for a few minutes to bait their horses and recruit their strength.

Walter rose that morning 'ere dawn in the pride of his heart, and big with stirring events upon which he was entering. He had dreamed of fresh conquests, and with dignity he paced his ancestral hall, while the spirit of his forefathers seemed to be afresh infused into his veins as he gazed on the shields there suspended, and at the pennons which had led the attack in many an affray.

"What dog is that," said he to the page who was fastening on his armour, "moaning at this time of morn ?"

"'Tis the lady Gertrude's, my lord. It is in her room. Shall I call her maid ?"

"That cannot be," said Walter harshly, "It would never growl were it with her.—Let us see."

He knocked at the door—there was no reply, but the pleasurable movements of the dog. He opened it—no Gertrude was visible. Immediately the cry was raised but no tidings answered it. Every room was searched, and Bertram was then missed. Walter was petrified. He reflected for a moment, then asked for the Palmer, who had been till then forgotten. His bed, also, was found—unoccupied.

"'Tis even so," exclaimed Walter, "the eagle has flown and robbed me of my dove.—Why did I not see it?" he added, as the intimacy between Gertrude and Bertram then rushed upon his mind.

"Holliday! where is Holliday! to horse with six of your stoutest horsemen; mount them well, and bring me my black charger. Now for the hoofs of the Strickland against the wings of the eagle!"

The horses were prepared for the foray, and almost as soon as ordered, Walter was hastening away. He was himself surprised at their speed as he signed his forehead on passing the cross erected about a mile from Kendal. No detention occurred in that town, and away they sped with a scent of the fugitives as plain as an almost unpeopled district could give.

Onward also had hurried the fugitives, and rapidly were they hastening to safety, when the merchant (in reality an attendant) fancied he heard the distant haloo of a huntsman. 'Twas even so, and they were pursued.

"By my faith," outspoke Bertram, "no darkness or delay has baffled them. 'Tis the weight of the trusty sword that must win the bonnie bird of Sizergh now."

"Is Walter there," asked Gertrude, "oh spare him, spare him for my sake." It was no moment for reply. —The horses were becoming fatigued.—A river was before them—in they dashed, and from the rising ground beyond they espied the pursuing force.

"Bertram," said the Palmer, "two miles hence are fresh horses, and an attendant—reach them, and you are safe."

"We cannot—they gain on us, we must bide the onset here."

"For your life, you must not stay," said the Palmer, —they are seven, and your only hope is for myself and Malcolm to hold them awhile at bay."

"You must not sacrifice your life for me," said Bertram.

"God's will be done," said the Palmer. "If you flee not with that lovely dame, every one must be destroyed; for never will I see her who has given herself to the Greame again in the fangs of the pursuer; this good sword shall sooner send her to the presence of the Blessed Virgin, than your pledge to your bride be annuled." Bertram listened and was determined. The Palmer and the attendant turned them in a narrow pass where they could not be flanked, to await the encounter, while the weary lovers urged onward their jaded steeds.

The hoofs of horsemen approached nearer, and into sight hurried Holliday, whose gallant grey was ever foremost in pursuit. Little expecting to find the quarry at bay, however, he was taken unawares. But could Will Holliday quail before a foeman?

"Never waver," said the soldier, and he dashed at the Palmer.

Then were the nerves of the horse and horseman nerved to their strength. Blow followed blow from their trusty falchions. The wounds of Holliday had already dyed the dapple of his charger. His sword was shivered, and he thurst with his dirk at the Palmer's heart.

Now, save thee, pilgrim! 'Twas even so,—his ex-

perienced sword has done its homage, and the helmet
of the yeoman, split by its force, left his brow unsheltered from the tremendous blow of the blade's descending edge. He fell. Alas, brave Holliday! the priests
must now say masses for the soul of one who had never
learned more than *ave maria* for himself. Two of his
companions shared his fate, and as Walter approached,
he, seeing the consequences of impetuous zeal, awaited
the arrival of two more of his attendants, and then led
them headlong to the attack.

He might have parleyed 'ere he drew sword on the
Palmer, but the blood of Holliday had unsanctified the
priest, and as lion meets lion, so met the enraged com-
batants. The struggle was unequal, but not long. The
Palmer's companion and Walter's two attendants were
stricken to the earth. The leaders, rendered furious
by the severity of the contest, again urged on their
steeds, and the shock of their meeting was like the
rush of the ocean tempest upon the rock. Their shivered swords were thrown away, and the fatal dirks glit-
tered in the sun. Weakened with loss of blood, the
Palmer's strength at last failed,—yet another deadly
blow and he bit the dust. The last lagging attendant found Walter wounded and dismounted reclining
upon the bank.

Where were then Gertrude and the Greame? With
agonising feelings they had hurried onwards,—fresh
horses quickened their speed,—and Gertrude safely deposited in a friendly tower, Bertram and a party of
attendants hastened back to the combat. What a
scene met his view. Bertram's blood ran chill when
the wounded and the dead, clotted in their gore, were
before him!

"Ah, Strickland," said he, "may God preserve you
for Gertrude's sake."

"Indeed," replied Walter, I am now your prisoner, but whether for life or death I know not, for the stalwart sword of that old Palmer has unnerved my strength."

"Old! call you him," said Bertram, "strip off his disguise and you will see as noble and gallant a knight as ever was brother to the Greame."

"Your Brother!"

"Yes," continued Bertram, throwing back the cowl and unfastening the artificial beard, and displaying a handsome and youthful warrior, "it is my brother, Reginald Greame!" and his feelings overpowered him.

Walter was conveyed to Lamplugh, where Gertrude, —now installed its lady by intervention of the Abbot of Holme Abbey, nursed him with a sister's love, related to him the plotting of the Government against Bertram's life, to her brother's infinite surprise and anger, who, when well enough to see the Greame, greeted him with thanks, and added, smiling,—

"The falchion of war shall be sheathed for awhile,
And the mild beams of peace o'er the border shall smile."

THE ANCHORITE'S WELL.

Years—ages—have passed away, and left scarcely a token of their flight, since the death of the recluse whose abode by its side first gave a distinctive name to this placid well; yet the spring still flows, fresh and pure as ever; and its name still lingers, and recalls many a day-dream of the far-off monastic times, when its translucent waters were deemed holy, and pilgrims came to drink them, and be cleansed from sin. We never pass the spot without reverence—not the super-stitious reverence of him who would revive observances which perished simply because the world had outgrown the belief of their efficacy—but the reverence of one who reflects that even superstitions form a part of the history of man, and are intimately connected with the progress of the human mind and the phenomena of human passions. We can calmly listen to stories of ghosts, witches, fairies, and of the escapades of hob-goblins, both because they have had credence in a darker age, and because they throw a light upon those indefinable workings of the imagination which still cling to us all, and form by no means the unpleasant-est part of our existence. Who is there among us that would put away the beautiful dreams he had in child-hood, of the elfin tribes that had their haunts in the green fields, and among the flowers, lurking in the cup of the lily, or dancing on the daisy's crest? If there be any such, he never felt the pure and tranquil de-

lights of poesy or music; never was enraptured with
beauty, for its own sake; and consequently never
tasted half the delights which this really lovely
world of ours is capable of affording to its inhabitants.

The age of "steam" and "utilitarianism" has
somewhat abridged the domain of the day-dreamer;
but fancy has its quiet nooks still ; and the *Anchorite's
Well*, "on the west side of Kirkland," in Kendal, is one
of them. Did you never pause, gentle reader, as you
wended past that or a similar spot, to wonder who was
the solitary being who first fixed his dwelling there,
and what was his story ?—for never yet did man se-
clude himself from the society of his fellows, but a story
of sadness and suffering was linked with his fate. Religious retirement and meditation have been sometimes
put forth as the motives which operate upon devotees
to become hermits; but we demur to this conclusion,
and place the items assigned in the category of consequences, instead of causes. A man may become a monk
from mere disgust with the world and its ways ; from
a belief that self-mortification may be acceptable to his
Maker; or from possessing a disposition which unfits
him for the jostle of every-day life; but he will pause
ere he become an anchorite—a lonely, friendless outcast—without occupation or affections—in fact, a breathing corpse.

We did not sit down, however, to philosophize but
to tell a story—the story of the identical hermit who
wore out the remnant of a life of sorrow and austerity
beside the *Anchorite's Well*. How we originally became acquainted with the facts—whether we read them
in some forgotten chronicle, or heard them from an
enthusiastic antiquary — catholic or protestant — or
merely dreamed of them, sleeping, or awake, is a mat-

ter concerning which we are totally oblivious; but on
this the reader may depend, that the tale is quite as
true as other legends, and indeed, as a great number of
romantic narratives which pass current through the
world, dignified with the graver title of Histories.

It was towards the end of the reign of King Edward
the Third that an Anchorite first constructed his cell
beside this living fountain. The recluse appeared in
Kendal, in the habit of a palmer, with the crossed staff,
the robe, and the broad, flat hat, decorated with a cockle
shell, which denoted that he had been in the holy-land.
Nobody enquired who or what the pilgrim was—for
the class was as common then, as commercial travellers
are at present. It was evident, however, that the stranger
was wealthy; for, though he lived on the humblest fare,
he bestowed much money in alms on the lepers and
licensed beggars who infested the highways, sat before
the cross-houses, or basked in the sunshine at the
church doors. He tarried in Kendal—contrary to the
wont of palmers—for some time; from spring to autumn,
wandering about the neighbourhood, but seldom accost-
ing or being accosted by any one. Yet it came afterwards to be observed that he daily visited the spring
which issued in the mead at the back of Kirkland, and
remained, as if musing, there, for some time. He was
a tall, stalwart man, and had been handsome; but the
burning sun of the East had withered his dark hair,
and tanned his forehead, across which premature
wrinkles were stealing in deep furrows.

As the leaves began to drop from the trees, the palmer busied himself in collecting stones from the Fell;
and having by the payment of a handsome sum to the
resident priesthood—brothers of the Abbey of St. Mary's
at York—obtained permission from the Church for that
purpose, he constructed himself a hovel, furnished it

with the rudest and simplest materials, and took up his
abode by the spring-side. His was a wretched dwelling; unsheltered alike from wind and wet—without
window or chimney; but there the palmer chose to
remain through the winter—fortifying himself from the
intrusions of bad weather, with clay and mud, as he
best might. He visited the town occasionally to procure provisions, which were always of the coarsest
kind; and he frequently attended church; but seldom
when there were other observers beside those who
officiated at the several, altars in the sacred edifice.

Curiosity began to be roused concerning the stranger.
He had changed his pilgrim's weeds, and laid aside his
staff; and had assumed a coarse white cossack of Kendal cloth—a manufacture which had recently been introduced into the town, from Flanders. His dwelling
was resorted to by those who sought to penetrate the
mystery which surrounded him; but as he neither encouraged nor repulsed those who came to gaze upon
him, and held not a word of communication with the
idlers, no eligible opportunity was afforded for eliciting
his secret. Father Ingelram was the name which he
had given to some children, set by their gossip mothers
to question him; and, as this was all that either urchins
or matrons could gather, Father Ingelram was the name
by which he was known. Many months elapsed ere
the craving of marvel-mongers, concerning the anchorite's history, subsided; but it did subside at last, like
all other ungratified appetites except hunger and thirst;
and then the hermit dwelt in his seclusion at peace.
He was always busy—cultivating the little patch of
ground attached to his cell—rendering his hovel more
commodious and better fenced, or in directing the sur-
plus water of the spring, which then began to be called
the *Anchorite's Well*, into a channel that might benefit

his neighbours in the street of Kirkland below. His
resources seemed never failing. He never desired cre-
dit, nor accepted alms; but had always a small sum in
his pouch to bestow upon such as he met in his occasional wanderings, who seemed to need charity.

Months—years—passed thus; and baffled curiosity
had given place to reverence. The anchorite was
deemed a holy man, and the spring became the resort
of the afflicted, who fondly thought that its pure waters
and the prayers of the hermit were capable of working
miracles. Perhaps, indeed, a kind of miracles were
sometimes wrought by Father Ingelram, for in his
journey to and from Palestine, and during his abode in
the East, he had gathered much knowledge in the heal-
ing art—which at that period was much better understood abroad than in England, and best of all among
the Saracen Arabs. But to any special gift of cure the
anchorite never pretended — attributing his success
whenever it was ascribed to *his* virtues, to the mere
virtues of the means which he had used to produce it.

At length he was suddenly missed from his accustomed place in the church, on his customary days of
attendance. No stir was made at first, for it was
deemed that his absence might have had its origin in
ordinary circumstances; but, as he was a liberal bene-
factor to the clergy, those who missed his donations
became uneasy, talked together of the oddity of the
thing, of the oddity of the man—wondered who and
what he could be—and finally resolved to satisfy themselves in full, by a visit to his cell. On re-considera-
tion it was decided that Brother Ralf the Confessor
should be deputed singly to attend him; and accordingly Brother Ralf presented himself, one summer's
evening, at the door of the hermitage.

He knocked. There was no answer. He lifted the

wooden latch—there was no lock on the door—and walked in. He paused—as most men will on entering a house where they are uncertain as to their reception, and listened. A faint sound from a small inner chamber struck his ear. It was a feeble attempt to articulate aloud, and was followed by a suppressed moan. Father Ingelram, it was evident, was sick.

Brother Ralf assumed confidence and went into the sleeping chamber of the Hermit. The good man was dying. He motioned the Confessor to administer some liquid standing on a rude table near his straw pallet, which he had been unable previously to reach; and having taken the cordial, he felt in some measure revived—sufficiently to express a wish to receive the consolations of the church—for he knew that his last hour was approaching. Brother Ralf was a kind and tender-hearted man, who, relishing life and its good things himself, sympathized heartily—when it in no degree affected his purse or personal comforts—with all who were about to quit the scene of "pomps and vanities;" so he readily did what he was requested, according to the forms prescribed by the Pope. The act of confession was brief, but it told the History of the dying man; and, agreeably to the desire of the anchorite, it was afterwards communicated by Brother Ralf to the chief of his Abbey. It may have lost much of its interest by transmission through successive generations: but, as preserved by tradition, thus it ran:—

"He who addresses you, Father, has been bowed to the grave by sorrow rather than by years. Thirty years ago I was still a youth—a boy—a reveller in splendid halls, sunning myself in the rays of beauty, and feeding on high hopes. It would be an idle story to tell you the dawning of a passion which proved the bane of my existence. I saw, and loved one whose grace and love-

D

liness were perfect as our conceptions of angels—perfect
as the forms bodied forth in the sculptures of that
Grecian land whither I wandered in maturer days.
She looked on, smiled upon, listened to me, shared my
dream of happiness, embroidered my scarf, and wrought
the blazon of my knightly pennon when I had won my
spurs by capturing a Scottish chief. We never spoke of
love—ours was no lip-worship;—our souls seemed to
have intermingled—to have been wedded, as it were by
instinct, and both were blessed.

"But I was called away to the wars; and Blanche
remained in her bower—not solitary; for I had a
brother to whom I committed her safety, and whom I
charged to be to her all that I had been. I returned,
but Blanche was no longer what she had been. Her
eye met mine with timidity; she did not shun, but she
ceased to seek me; she would not wander with me alone,
as of old, by stream and woodland, on the mountain's
side, or through the quiet vales. I sought an explanation from my brother, but obtained only evasive an-
swers. I watched, in order to draw conclusions from
circumstances; and jealousy, rage, frenzy, soon took
possession of my breast. Blanche had given her heart
to my brother—had pledged her faith to be his bride.
I stifled my resentment for a time, but I brooded over
their falsehood in secret; and, like a pent-up fire, my
wrath gathered strength and grew more fierce from
concentration. One evening, Sir Priest,—we were then
staying for a time at Kendal Castle,—Blanche and her
lover had wandered forth into the balmy air, to breathe
the odours of spring. I saw them from my lonely turret chamber—followed them—it grew dusk—I drew
sufficiently near to hear their words, which fell like arrows on my heart. My brother dared to jest with his
betrothed on the fatal passion which he knew to be

consuming me. I heard no more, but rushed upon
him with my dagger. Blanche threw herself upon his
neck to shield him from my violence, and both, in the
same instant—by the same blow—were transfixed in
death.

"Fear then succeeded to frenzy. I procured means to
conceal the bodies. I buried them, Father, beside
this well. Lift the stone, that with the ring at the
foot of my couch, and you will find the coffin in which
their remains still moulder. No one guessed their fate,
and least of all could they have imagined that I had
been their destroyer. They had fled, and were heard
of no more. Long was their return looked for; but in
vain. They slept the sound sleep of death; and I—
was their murderer!

"But think you, when my revenge was satiated,
that the fever of my heart and brain abated? Remorse
clung to me. Two phantoms incessantly haunted me;
twining together as in mortal agony like the beings I
had slain. They haunt me yet. At dawn, at noon,
in the twilight, amid drear darkness, they are ever
present—ever visible. Asleep or waking I cannot be
released from the spell of their glowing eyes and quivering lips. I am dying, Father; but I feel that they
will still confront and accuse me in the grave.

"I disposed of my patrimony when it devolved on
me, to a relative, and assumed the Cross, hoping to
leave my burden of guilt at the foot of Mount Calvary.
I have traversed Palestine; have fought against the
Infidels; bestowed my wealth in alms, and acts of
charity; but the curse of the murderer is still graven
deeply on my brow. On my return, I could not control my yearnings to revisit the scene of my crime. I
was attracted hither. I built this hermitage; opened
the grave of the dead, and gazed upon their relics.

Here I have since lived, here I shall die, and here I seek to be buried.   My name is Julian de Clifford. Can the Church absolve me ?''

Brother Ralf boggled at an answer ; but the penitent gave the worthy priest to understand that there were money bags in store for masses, and that the Church was to inherit all that the hermit had hoarded; so Ralf did the needful ; and found, when he had concluded, that De Clifford's soul had taken flight.

We have never heard how much of the anchorite's treasure Brother Ralf retained to himself, nor how much he dispensed in charity ; but masses for the soul of Julian de Clifford continued to be celebrated in Kendal Church till the period of the Reformation.

THE CASTLE WATCH.

The autumn sun had been set about two or three hours, and the harvest-moon was riding high in the heavens; but Adam Winton and his comrades, as they kept watch and ward on the ramparts of Kendal Castle, found the night chilly, and often paused at the flagon of ale which was kept reaming for their special use within. The knightly house of Parr was not niggardly to its dependents and retainers, and it was served with the greater cheerfulness by its vassals on that account. Adam Winton had been born a servant of the Parrs,—had grown up on their estate, —had seen much service on their account upon the borders and in Scotland,—and being now somewhat grey-headed, and withal a brave and skilful soldier, was esteemed an oracle among his younger brethern in arms. Adam was good humoured too, and loved a merry tale, a jest and a song ; and deplored, like many others of his day and calling, the introduction and general adoption of "machinery" in the noble art of war. The cannon he said—he had heard it somewhere from those who had caught the phrase in the south—was the tomb of valour, and the fire-lock the sexton of a good soldier ; and as nobody disputed Adam's word on such matters, cannon and firelock were anathematised by all who were bound to do duty on the summit of the castle hill.

But we are wandering from our tale—just as old
Adam used to do; and, like him, we must bring ourselves, by an effort, back to the starting point.

It was near midnight then, and the lights had, one
by one, disappeared from the windows of the baronial
apartments situate over and about the grand entrance
of the castle ; and, though the autumn was not far advanced, the night wind soughed heavily round the time-
worn battlements, and struck chilly to the faces and
bosoms of the warriors who stalked around the solemn
inclosure.   By degrees the whole watch stood collected
within the tower in which were the ale-cans. It might
be a neglect of duty perchance, to leave the grey walls
thus to take care of themselves ; but the brave Earl of
Surrey was at that time beyond the border, and news
had been received of the battle of Flodden, and the
death of the gallant though hostile Scottish King ; so
Adam thought there could be little danger of surprisal
from that quarter; and he knew that there could be
none from his countrymen ; for his master had not a
foe, no, nor a feud, in the land.   Adam almost regret-
ted that it was so; but so it was, and the retainers of
the Parrs were condemned to a life of inactivity in
consequence.

The ale passed freely from hand to hand, and jests,
followed fast and ever faster upon each other in the old
circular watch room ; the peat fire glowed brightly in
the centre, and imparted a swarthier hue to the swar-
thy faces of those collected around it, who talked and
laughed at their own and their kinsmen's achievements
of yore, both in the tented field and the bower of beauty.
Each had his ready tale—not always the worse for
having been revised during the progress of some score
of previous recitals ; but the tale of Adam Winton
was the most marvellous of all ; and so much the more

zest it had that not one of his comrades had heard whisperings concerning the facts of which it treated, and each knew that Adam, if he would, could narrate the full particulars.

When each had exhausted his little stock of anecdotes there came a pause in the conversation, as there will always ensue under like circumstances in the best and wittiest societies,—and, during this, Adam looked out upon the night, and saw that a dim cloud had drawn near to the moon. There was nothing in that circumstance, it might be supposed, to awaken gloomy reflections. Moonshine, the real and imaginary, are often obscured by clouds, which are fully as obnoxious to the mere "castle builder," as to the watcher on a castle wall,—yet, common as clouds are, the particular cloud of which Adam Winton caught a glimpse on that particular night, not only called up a train of dismal recollections within him, but loosened the old man's tongue.

"It was this night twenty years," said Adam, "that Simon Bell died."

"Indeed," said young Walter Dickson, "and what did that portend?"

Walter was rather a favourite of Adam Winton's, for he was a skilful youth with the long bow, and had won several prizes at wrestling and hurling the bar; but Adam deemed his question irreverent, and answered it only by a *look*. Walter, abashed, retreated a step from the fire, and Adam resumed :—

" Twenty years ago this night, died Simon Bell. I knew Simon for twenty years before that; and once heard, from his own mouth, the story of his misadventure with the fairies."

Everyone opened both his ears at this announcement; for every one believed in fairies, though none had ever yet been satisfied of their existence by ocular demonstration.

"Simon," continued the stalwart Winton, after another long pull at the can, for he disdained the luxury of a drinking horn, "Simon had been to Ambleside,— it was this day forty years, though it then fell on a Friday,—a fine autumn day—just as this day has been. He had been seeing a few friends, and, may be, making free with their beverage ; for Simon was sociable, and never shirked his part either at the bow, the bar, or the barrel ; but still he was sober—I had it from his own mouth, and most particular I was to get at the truth of that matter ; for I was a little incredulous as to the story he told me, till after events had confirmed it. Rest his soul! he was a little nettled that I should entertain a doubt concerning the strength of his head to bear potations of double strength to what a man of these degenerate days would stagger under. But sober he was, without doubt, and so it was proved in the sequel.

"He had made it somewhat late ere he thought of returning :—but as he was under-steward here at the castle, never much was said about Simon's outgoings or incomings ; and besides, Sir William, our noble master's father, was then but newly married to the Lady Fitzhugh, and had pleasanter things to think about than the loiterings of Simon Bell. When he did set out homeward, however, both he and his nag were desirous of accomplishing the journey in double-quick time; and came on at a rate which would have done your heart good to see. But by the time they had reached Staveley, the moon, which had before been shining as brightly as it did to-night, became obscured, precisely as it now is; and Simon and his beast then seemed to have less confidence in themselves, and in

each other, than they had under the broad glare of
light in which they had previously been proceeding.
Simon, indeed, grew bewildered; and so it appeared
did his steed ; for all at once the beast stood stock still
at a cross-road, and snorted and jerked as if she wished
to turn back; but Simon held her tight in, and kept
her head toward home. As he looked round, however,
to see what might have occasioned the brute's unusual
obstinacy, he saw—"

Adam paused once more for a draught of the strong
October; and perchance,—for our ancestors understood
quite as well as ourselves the arts of oratory,—to excite
the impatience of his auditors : but if such was his intention he did not long leave them to the dominion of
wonder.

"He saw," resumed Adam, "a band of dry-bellied,
lantern-visaged Scots, all below the middle stature, all
dressed in tartan, and all carrying meagre rush lights
in their hands, as if about to traverse a moss, and uncertain as to finding the road. Tramp they came along
the bye-road as noiselessly as if their clog-soles had
been purposely made of felt. The sight was an unusual
one, and Simon at once divined that it was a clan from
the borders, and that mischief must needs ensue. He
looked around him on every hand, but no beacon was
blazing. He looked before him, and there were the
stealthy Scots—tramp—tramp—tramping along—without bagpipe or music—without sound of foot or of voice.
Simon drew back at sight of the array, and cowering by
the hedge-side, crossed himself more than once ; for he
thought his last hour had come, or that at least he was
doomed to an indefinite term of captivity : but on went
the dim procession, regardless alike of him and his
beast. Presently, however, a little old gentleman in a
large bonnet that at first concealed his features, came

E

forth from the ranks and accosted him. What the little being said, Simon never knew; supposing however that he wanted some money, Simon fumbled for the pouch that he wore at his girdle; but his hand trembled, and the pouch itself seemed to have vanished. He sought to crave mercy; but his tongue clave to the roof of his mouth, and he was unable to utter a syllable. He looked down imploringly upon the little old gentleman, and as the latter raised his head, he perceived that he had two horns on his forehead, eyes set round with fiery eyelashes, a tail whisking nimbly under his kilt, and a couple of cloven feet for supporters. It was a fearful moment for a man who had not lately received absolution. Simon grew desperate. His nag made a plunge into the thick of the throng, and in an instant Simon was stricken from the beast's back, and lay a helpless burden in the road, deprived of sense and motion. How long he lay thus he never knew; but when he awoke, his horse and the Scots troopers were all gone, and he had to walk, cold and numbed, to the castle; where, taking a long draught of strong ale to revive him, he went to bed and slept soundly till mid-day.

"Simon, when he arose, was questioned; and he questioned every body in return, as to the proceedings of the Scots; but nothing could ever be heard of them, and nothing could ever be guessed as to their meaning or intentions, until the good chaplain, who was confessor to my Lady, suggested that it was a ' raid of the fairies,' and was meant for a token."

"And Simon's horse?" inquired Walter Dickson, who had gathered confidence again since his former rebuke; "What became of the horse?"

"It was a mare," answered Adam testily. "Nothing became of her. She was found next morning grazing quietly in the castle park at the foot of the hill."

"And you think," said sturdy old Hugh Morton, at this juncture, "that Simon was sober?"

"Sober as our priest, saving his reverence," replied Adam; "and this was proved by what followed. That year a raid from the kilted scarecrows out o' the land o' girdles was made; they came on the town in the night, and before morning every house was gutted; seven maidens were taken into the border erie; and there was not a cow left for miles round; the year was also famous for murrain among the Westmorland cattle; all the October in Kendal and hereabouts was spoiled by mildews and thunder; the fat buttery-maid at the castle-dairy died the same night, and Dick Heversham's wife the next Wednesday—though they did say that Dick did not fret much for that—for his wife wore the nether garments. The fairies—if they were nothing worse—it is clear must have been Scots fairies; and their object was doubtless to avenge themselves for some slight put upon them by the English borderers in one of their forays. Besides haven't I told you that Simon Bell himself died that day twenty years."

"And that's twenty years ago?" replied Walter Dickson.

"This blessed night," added Adam, "and may-be there are fairies stirring now—if we had only been out like Simon Bell and his steed, and had taken sufficient October to enable us to see them."

BURNESIDE HALL.

It has been well said by our fine old poet, Webster,

" I do love these ruins ;
One never treads upon them, but we set
Our feet upon some reverend history."

Who is there that has passed Burneside Hall without feeling that a venerable page of history lay open
before him in those mouldering towers; and that he
had obtained a glimpse into the past, such as no mere
book-lore could afford him ? To acquire this feeling it
is not necessary that a man should be acquainted with
the local history of the place, or the names and genea-
logy of its ancient occupants. The desolate chambers,
the crumbling walls, the rapid and tinkling burn that
murmurs sweet music at his feet, the ruined steps and
turrets, the very ivy clinging to the fabric which cher-
ished it of old, seeming to be still desirous of recalling
a dream of its youth, have tales with which every heart
must sympathise ; tales of wealth and power, of glory,
of pomp and of happiness ; of ambition, love, disappointment and sorrow. We linger round such rem-
nants of departed years with a sort of yearning to
penetrate the veil which succeeding generations have
thrown over the life and manners of our forefathers ;
and when, by any lucky chance, we are enabled to lift
a corner of the mystic covering, we brood over the
scene that presents itself with the fondness of an antiquary gloating over the mummy of King Pharoah of
Egypt, or the coffin of Alexander the Great.

The hall of Burneside is one of those romantically situated fortalices with which Westmorland and all the border counties abound ; and its history, as preserved in recorded annals, is, like that of most similar places, brief and meagre; but it has a further and more interesting history in tradition. The Burnesheads, the Bellinghams, and the Brathwaites are restored to us at the cottage fireside, and in the chimney nook of the rustic farmer,—whose ancestors have tilled the same fields and tended the same flocks from the days of Bannockburn, to the moment in which we are writing —as beings of flesh and blood, with heads to devise, hearts to urge, and hands to execute high and great achievements—with human passions and feelings, to exalt, to rejoice, or to sadden and instruct us.

We have a winter tale of Burneside Hall—a tale of the merry Christmas—of the days when *Hobthrust*, the fairy, was more than a mere imaginary being; and when the now peaceful and intelligent Scots were a wild and lawless race, holding the country side in fear, and often converting the homesteads of the Westmorland yeomen into beacons, to warn the neighbourhood of approaching ravage and desolation.

The hall of which we speak was occupied at the time of our homely story, by Gilbert de Burneshead, a bold and loyal knight, who had done good service in the reign of Edward the 1st., both in Palestine and on the Northern borders, and who, in the reign of the weak-minded second Edward, obtained the Hall and its demesnes, as a reward for rescuing the coward monarch from the hands of his enemies in the disastrous flight before the Bruce from Stirling. Gilbert had an only daughter, Margaret, who had known little of a mother's care or tenderness—that parent having been taken from her ere she had reached her seventh year. But

Margaret, nevertheless, had been carefully brought up
in the south, with relatives to whom her orphan state
had endeared her, and who had esteemed her as their
own ; insomuch indeed that she had borne their name
during her stay in their household, and when she quitted their hospitable roof to be the stay and solace of
her father at Burneside, she felt for a time as if she
had been rent from home. The sweet and peaceful
vale of the Darent in Kent, with its rich orchards and
green meadows, its undulating hills and placid streams,
accorded with her gentle nature far better than the
magnificent mountains and turbulent waters of the
North ; and there was perhaps another remembrance
of a still tenderer and dearer nature, linked with
thoughts of the South, which made the hills of Westmorland seem more bleak, and its inhabitants more
wild and strange than they would have appeared to a
less prejudiced beholder. Margaret was eighteen years
of age when she quitted Kent ; and she had returned
to the North not quite heart-whole. She had walked
through the meads of Hutton, had danced on the green
at Lullingstone Castle, and sat at the festive board
at Frants, with a youthful cavalier of the gallant
house of Herbert ; and though she had never dreamed of love when he was present, a sigh would swell
unbidden, and a teardrop start, when she thought,
as she often did, of the long and dreary space now
cast between her and the champion of her girlhood ;
and that she should never see the vale of Darent more.
Still Margaret did not repine. She loved her father,
and had been taught implicit obedience as a condition of her life ; and she had constant occupation, in
attention to her new duties as mistress of a mansion
which was filled with serving men and women, with
warlike retainers, and with guests, who, under the

almost boundless hospitality of the period, came and
departed from the hall at pleasure. She entertained
somewhat of melancholy and regret, it might be. That
was natural. The dream of her youth had been interrupted at the moment of its most abundant beauty,—
and when she looked round upon the warriors and
chieftains who formed the circle of her father's friends,
she could not avoid contrasting them with the gay and
gallant "Squire of the bugle," as the handsome nephew
of Sir Alan Herbert had been called, amid more congenial and familiar scenes. Her father, however, had
a gentle heart beating under his steel breast-plate—at
least towards women, and such as were defenceless, and
most especially towards his child. The bravest perhaps are always the tenderest also; and Margaret was
content, for his sake, to spend her days amid the lonely
hills of Westmorland, and to be the gracious hostess of
their border chivalry.

A time of peace had followed the victory of Bruce at
Bannockburn, during which Sir Gilbert de Durneshead
occupied himself in the chace, in improving his Hall
and manor, and in the usual sports and employments
of an age which offered little that the existing race of
Englishmen would care to consider as pastime. The
"good old times," indeed, were somewhat of a cast-iron
character, in more respects than as regarded the armour
of its knights and soldiers; but its pleasures, notwithstanding, were pleasures in their day; and to blame or
stigmatise them now, would be to assume that the feelings and enjoyments of man were as immutable as the
nature of the streams and woods amid which his generations have flourished and decayed; a thing to which
all history offers a contradiction.

The peace of which we have spoken was of short
duration. The King, whose mind had been ruined by

the vicious indulgencies of a licentious Court, and by the attainment of uncontrolled power in mere boyhood, soon displayed his own unfitness to govern; and, by the choice of his ministers, forced his nobles to revolt. Burneshead with his followers took arms, among others, against the crown. Piers Gaveston fell a victim to the rage of those whom he had insulted and defied; but the imbecile Edward never forgave the authors of his humiliation. He contrived to thrust into authority a new minion — named Spenser; whose efforts were speedily directed to ruin those who had been engaged in contest with his master. Spies were employed; and it was discovered that the lord of Burneshead, unmindful of what was called "a pardon for his former treason," had lately afforded refuge to a newly declared traitor, and still retained his friendship and intercourse with those who looked with evil eyes upon the actions of the King.

Summoned to London to answer for his dereliction, old Gilbert stoutly refused to quit his mansion, till at length a messenger arrived to inform him that he had been attainted for contumacy, and that his estates had been forfeited, and given to another. It was a sad blow to the old chief, not so much for himself, for he was a soldier, and though his locks were white, his arm was still strong and his courage unabated; and he felt that he might yet have passed over to Ireland, and won a new renown and fortune under the brave brother of the Scottish king, who was then seeking to erect for himself a kingdom in the green Isle. But when he looked upon the fair face of his daughter Margaret, his heart failed, and his lip quivered; and he pressed the maiden to his bosom in silence—resolved to abide the worst rather than quit her, or to lead her amid scenes of lawless strife. The father and the daughter were all in all to each other. He had none to love—none to love him—but her; and misfortune, though it could not tame his proud spirit, added depth and breadth to his affections.

He sued for pardon, humbled himself before the low-born and vulgar-minded Hugh Spensor, and obtained a felon's grace—his life. He forfeited manors and farms, his hall and vassals had been transferred, under the royal signet, to a favourite of the bold and gay young Prince of Wales, Sir Richard Bellingham, of Tynedale. Still no one came to claim the wide domain. Day after day went on, and Gilbert lingered at the Hall of Burneside, re-visiting anew every spot that could bring to him a recollection of past pleasures—no longer, however, acting as a chief—though still regarded as such by his followers; but still day by day taking leave, as it were, of home, to renew his familiarity with it, and to be found the same man, in all but his ancient confidence and glee, on the morrow.

Thus summer passed, and autumn was waning, when one evening, as Margaret was pacing the terrace, over-looking the burn head, with its wooded islands, a horse-man in gay attire rode up to the Hall by the approach from Kendal, knocked at the wicket of the arched gate-way, and demanded to see the aged knight. The occurrence was not an unusual one, so Margaret pursued her walk and her meditations without asking a question. Those who have loved, and felt the spell of a tranquil autumn eve upon the heart, in absence, will be at no loss to trace the wanderings of her thoughts to a dis-tant vale, where stood the hall in which she had pass-ed such happy days of girlish pleasure, and to the "squire of the bugle" with his merry laugh, his light-hearted song, and his bold bearing in the chivalrous tourney. A wild and fond fancy however suddenly

F

flashed upon her mind as she paced the quiet rampart.
The messenger might have brought intelligence from
him who occupied her thoughts. His accent and habit
were those of the south, and his steed seemed travel-
wearied. She indulged and rejected the thought a hundred times—it might almost be said in a minute, so
rapid are the transitions of the excited mind; but ere
she had finally dismissed her conjectures she was summoned to her father's presence by her bower-maiden.

The old man had gone to her apartment in search of
her, and now sat there alone with downcast eye and
head. He had never yet ventured to break the news of
his disinheritance in a definite or coherent manner to his
daughter: for he could not brook the thought of bring-
ing the knowledge of misery to her until the duty should
be forced upon him. The moment had now arrived.

"Margaret," said the old man, after preparing her to
hear tidings of sorrow, "We must quit this hall."

"My father?" said the maiden enquiringly, not com-
prehending the intimation.

"It has been forfeited to the King," replied Gilbert;
"and he, unmindful that I saved his craven life when
he was fleeing from the catterans beyond the border,
has exacted the penalty."

"Be it even so, my father," said the damsel; "we
shall find a pleasanter home in the south, among our
kindred."

"Nay, Margaret," returned the old man, "I have
grown gray among these vales and mountains; I have
ever lived as mine own master, and feasted at my own
board. I cannot now part, without a pang, from all
that—"

Is there, then, no way to avert the consequences?"

"I see none. Yet—"

"Yet what, my father?"

"This missive, which our chaplain has just read to me, and the terms of which thou wilt see, contains a proposal to which I would willingly accede, should it not mar thy hopes of happiness."

Margaret took the strip of parchment tendered her, glanced hastily through its contents, rested her flushed brow for a moment on her hand, then, saying that she would return an answer in an hour, arose and left the apartment.

The weight of that long hour oppressed Sir Gilbert as would an age of solitary inactivity. He sat rivetted to his silken-cushioned stool, like one without the power of motion, his mind roaming from his daughter to his broad lands, and thence to the ancient Church of Kendal, in which his forefathers had their tombs and monuments, and in which he had hoped that his own remains would be laid when his earthly race should be ended. He loved his daughter too well to force her will; yet, at the same time, he felt that the demand of young Bellingham for her hand, as the price of his hall and estates, was such as, in the judgment of every person in that day, would be considered both generous and noble:—such as he himself might have urged, in pure good-will and sincerity, ere he had wedded the daughter of Sir Thomas de Chenaye.

On her return, the father saw that Margaret had been weeping.

"It shall not be," said the old man tenderly. "We will away, my girl, to-morrow."

"Nay—my father, I am not so childish, or so light of faith. I have given the messenger of Bellingham my assent; and he is already mounting his steed in the Court to depart to-night. Having orders, he says, to speed at once with his answer to Kenilworth, where the young prince now holds his Court."

Sir Gilbert pressed his lips to his daughter's forehead, and a tear trickled from his sun- browned cheeks to hers. It was a response more eloquent than words : and went far to compensate her for what she could not but feel, nevertheless, was a sacrifice to parental affection.

The nuptials were fixed to take place at Christmas, and preparations were urged forward for the event, with as much glee and hilarity, among those who knew not that there was a tale concealed, as if an union of hearts had been contemplated as well as of hands. Sir Gilbert, however, was melancholy, testy, and occasionally morose towards his faithful followers, a sort of conduct which, in him, who had always been a kind and beloved master, was utterly unaccountable ; and Margaret instead of being elated, as maidens generally are, at the near prospect of their own bridal, grew more and more depressed as the day drew nigh. It was a mystery, and came to be spoken of as such in hall and kitchen ; but it was one which none could penetrate, except the Knight, his daughter, and their mutual confessor.

To tell how with her, who was most concerned, eve succeeded to morn, and matins to vespers, as Christmas-tide drew on, would be idle. She saw the chapel decked for the cheerful though solemn celebration, the hall glittering with the bright green leaves and glistening berries of the holly, interspersed with mystic misletoe ; the neighbouring barons and knights—the Stricklands and Cliffords, and Veteriponts and Leyburnes—had been invited to the high festival ; and there was to be mirth and rejoicing with all, except her whose heart felt at once hollow and heavy. She tried to banish the phantom of the handsome Kentish " Squire of the bugle" which haunted her ; but it was ever present to her eyes. She anathematized the

" Silent Darent stained with Danish blood !"

But it would flow, clear and placidly, before her, in place of the Kent and the Sprint, and seemed even to intrude itself between the lowly banks of the nameless burn that washed the foundations of the Hall in which she dwelt. Her head grew fevered, and her cheek pale, from the continual wear of thought and anxiety; insomuch that on Christmas eve—the day before the expected arrival of the bridegroom and his retinue—she could scarcely venture to quit her bower, but sat there moody and cheerless all day, listening to the bustle and revelry and preparation below, and calculating the long years to come of joyless, loveless wedlock. She only came forth at night-fall into the carved gallery to give some directions; but—oh, joy! what vision burst upon her sight, as she approached the stair-head to call her maiden. He of whom she had dreamed so long in hopelessness was before her; her father tottering behind—not in gladness of heart; for he knew not the welcome his guest and son-in-law elect would receive, but hastening to sustain his child through the trial which he deemed to await her. And Margaret needed sustaining in that moment, for her heart was full to overflowing. Sir Richard de Bellingham was her own "Squire of the Bugle," the light-hearted joyous nephew of the Kentish Herberts, and he had secured the fortune, after having won the heart, of the dark-eyed heiress of Burneside, who had never previously learned his name.

Long and loud were the Christmas revels that year at Burneside Hall; unchecked and uncontrolled was the dominion of the " lord of misrule" for his twelve days reign and a bittock, and bountiful was the largess of the Carolers and minstrels who gathered from far and near to add to the hilarity of the season and the event. Cottagers and vassals too had store of good cheer in their homes; and all rejoiced at the nuptials of the knight and his bride. Old Sir Gilbert, instead of sinking, as he had anticipated, into his grave in a month or two, lived long enough to teach one grandson the use of the lance and the broadsword, and to be kept in terror by the gambols of another, while fixed to his seat with the gout, like "a fine old English gentleman" who had enjoyed the drama of life, notwithstanding some rough squeezing, to the end.

SECOND EPOCH.—PART I.

The evening of New-Year's-Day had arrived, and Helen Bellingham had frequently started at the pattering rain which the gust hurled against the lancet windows of an upper room in Burneside Hall, fancying that she heard the tread of horses. Her father had promised to reach home on that day from London, and the anxious and affectionate daughter was watching in her own apartment, whose illuminated window she wished to serve as a guiding star to Sir Allan and his attendants.

Allan Bellingham had been for ten years a widower; yet Helen's solicitous affection and concern for his comfort had done much to supply his loss.

Weary with fruitless expectation, she descended to the large apartment which fronted the inner court, where lounged on a long-settle, her only brother.

"Godfrey," said she, addressing him, "mishap must have befallen the travellers; already has the horologe struck its hammer ten times, and I hear nought but the wild whistling of the wind amidst the trees and turrets."

"Fancy, fancy, girl, has diminished thy customary fortitude, and made thee anticipate change too soon," replied the careless youth.

With an indolence of temper, and an affection for associates beneath him, Godfrey had at the core, a feeling heart; and those who knew him best had long encouraged him to enter the service of some foreign baron — England being now at peace—in order to stimulate him to energy, by new scenes and motives. To their urgent remonstrances Godfrey had always replied, "When my liege lord wants a knight, the pennon of the Bellinghams shall be first at the muster; but never shall my blood flow for the pay of a mercenary."

Another hour passed, and the youth himself, though unwilling to confess it, became anxious. "Hark," said he, "if I mistake not the sound, a horse and his rider are at hand."

No other ear heard aught save the howling blast, but his was tutored to catch distant sounds, in hunting the red deer on Goatscar and Nanbield. "'Tis Gilpin's horse," he said, and opened the massive door. In rushed the tempest, and for a moment extinguished their candles. Godfrey snatched a brand from the hearth, and found the horseman at the gate.

"For Heaven's sake, bring lights and help, for our master is drowning in the ford," said Gilpin, and turned and galloped back, while Godfrey followed at his utmost speed. Helen rushed out almost bewildered, but recalling to mind the demand for lights, she summoned the servants, who procured links and torches, with which they hurried to the ford of the blessed Virgin, or as it was briefly termed, "our Lady's Ford." Great was Helen's joy on arriving at the scene of disaster, to find that her parent had been saved, and was

now sufficiently recovered to be anxiously watching
over the figure of a young man, evidently just extricated from the water. Godfrey was chafing his chest ; not
a word was spoken, lest the least symptom of returning
breath should be suppressed.

" Alas ! it is over," said he.

" For Heaven's sake, try a little longer Godfrey,"
urged his father. He did, and was rejoiced to find his
reward in success. So soon as animation was at all apparent, the almost lifeless corpse was carefully borne to
the hall, where proper remedies soon completed his
restoration.

It was not long before Helen, joyful in her father's
happy deliverance, had learned that the stranger was
her cousin, Reginald Duckett, of Grayrigg Hall. His
father had married Sir Allan's sister, and died while
Reginald was a youth. As heir to a large property, he
had been wandering in other countries, and visiting the
capital of his own Island, which at that period was the
most polished and chivalric of chivalric courts. Avail-
ing himself of his uncle's return to travel down with
him, he had accepted the invitation to rest at that late
hour of the night at Burneside, and in crossing the
ford, which had been suddenly swollen by the melted
snow drifts in the hills, Sir Allan was overborne by the
stream, and would inevitably have perished, had not
Duckett fearlessly dashed in, and, being an expert
swimmer, saved his uncle, though at the risk of his
own life. Wearied with buffeting the torrent, the rapid
stream was carrying him down, when the attendants
contrived to bring him to land.

The winter's sun had not risen with its lurid light,
over the ridge of Holm End, on the following morning,
when Helen, having already learned at her parent's
door, and, through Gilpin's intervention, at Duckett's,

that the accident of last night had left no ill effect upon
either, proceeded to the breakfast-room. Under her
direction, the table soon offered a substantial invitation
to all comers. The roast beef and boiled capons smoking from the kitchen, hot ale and piles of bread, oaten
porridge and honey, abundantly testified to the hospitality and the tastes of the period. Helen's welcome
to her cousin was artless and affectionate. He had
saved a parent's life, and she could not but be grateful.
She carried herself without restraint, for she dreamed
of no latent feeling that might spring from her gratitude. She had always viewed herself as engaged. Her
father had bestowed her in early youth on the son of
his friend, Sir Charles Leyburne, of Cunswick Hall.
Roger de Leyburne had been awaiting his acquisition
of property—an essential preliminary to his marriage
—when his father's death had suddenly occurred. He
now possessed ample means, and was petitioning Helen
to name an early day for that event.

A few days after this period, Leyburne, hearing of
Sir Allan's return, rode over to visit him, and received
a hearty welcome from the stout old knight. Their
conversation naturally turned on the death of Leyburne's father.

"I have often wished," said Sir Allan, "to hear
more particulars of your poor father's death. The
King's writ required my immediate presence in Parliament, and amid the bustle of preparation, the exact
circumstances are rather indistinct in my memory.
Poor fellow—in him we have lost a brave and tender-
hearted gentleman."

"You know," replied Roger, "that the sad event
took place on our return from visiting you. It was a
dismal evening—you pressed us to remain all night,
and my father inclined, but I knew that all here were

busy, in the hurry of your departure, and, therefore,
persuaded him to hasten home,—aye, and many a
sleepless night has my bed witnessed on that account
since."—"Yes, I recall it all distinctly: alas, Sir
Charles ! the thunder pealed its hollow groanings
amongst the hills, and the lightning seemed to rive
the black clouds in twain—'twas a night only fit for
demons :—but proceed—I interrupt you."—"When we
left your door, my soul misgave me; but onward we
went, only discerning the horse-track when the fire
blazed in heaven. We, however, safely reached that
point (you know it well) where a bend in the
river has washed away the bank, and the defenceless
cliff frowns over the dark stream. 'Twas there—perhaps the horse slipped—but that I know not for certain, when a cry from my father, who was following
me, arrested my attention—his horse rushed past, and
almost forced me over the edge. Crash, crash down
the cliff—and my eye just caught his grey hairs streaming in the wind, as the red lightning made night visible, then a hollow plash sounded, and all was darkness.
I was astounded, and galloped off for help—our search
was hopeless, and, though every pains were subsequently taken, we have never been able to discover the
body."

He ceased. Sir Allan was in deep thought, mourning for the friend of his boyhood. At last he said,
" Would to God and the mother of Jesus, that Sir
Charles had enjoyed christian burial. Roger, what
monks are saying masses for his soul ?"

" None, as yet," replied the young man.

" What ! thou undutiful son, shall thy father's soul
endure the pangs of purgatory, when he has left such
coffers of gold behind him ? But 'tis strange—'tis
passing strange. 'Twas not a month before his death

that he told me that your family had always enjoyed
holy sepulture; and some holy man had foretold that,
though often in the battle-field, still every Leyburne
should repose in the bosom of our mother church, until
one should arise whose self-destroyed corpse should
waste on the rocky fell overhanging Cunswick Hall. It
cannot be—but that I shall yet follow the remains of
my friend to the tomb of his fathers in Wensleydale."
—"It is impossible," said Roger, with a countenance
whose gathering darkness the old knight observed not.
"'Tis impossible! and as for the masses—why I cannot
make a bargain with those avaricious priests, and never
will I be overreached, even by a cowl-covered head."

"Aye, Sir," said Bellingham, but mark—the devil
sometimes wears a cowl; and would to heaven that so
clad he may never beguile you."

Bellingham soon retired to bed. He had heretofore
little observed the character of his future son-in-law—
the heir of his earliest friend :—but now he fancied that
he could see some dark traits therein, and he bethought
him that Sir Charles had once said, when talking of
the nuptials of their children, " True, Roger is a way-
ward lad, but your gentle Helen will tame him to goodness." He, however, had irrevocably pledged his
daughter's hand, and so he banished further anxiety
with the reflection that "the unspotted hind is not in
the deer park," and sleep soon set thought at rest.

Helen had also parted from Leyburne, who, while
chatting awhile with Godfrey in the hall, awaiting his
horse, heard the voice of singing. It was soft and
solemn. " What is that?" said his future brother-in-
law.

Oh, 'tis only Helen at her vespers!" said Godfrey,
" but you will not find a sweeter songster in Westmorland,—aye, though she is my sister I say it—Hark ye!"

They listened while Helen sang—

Holy Virgin ! low before thee
Bends a suppliant maiden now ;
Spread thy safe protection o'er me ;
Seal with peace my slumbering brow.

Stars now shining bright above me,
Witnessed once the pangs thou bore ;
When a Saviour came to love me,
And my wandering soul restore.

By thy suffering I implore thee,—
By the love thou bore thy Son,—
Oh, most blessed, I adore thee—
Help me sin and shame to shun !

Then, though tempests gather round me,
Sun-be-dimmed, and dark my sky,
Heavenly care shall still surround me,
While I in thy bosom lie.

She ceased—Gilpin announced that the horse was at
the door, and Roger, with a hasty good bye, vaulted
into his saddle, and sped homeward.

The moon shone bright as she ploughed her way
among the fleecy clouds. Sometimes dense masses of
rock hid her beaming face, at others day light itself
might have vied with the silvery brilliancy of the illuminated scene. Leyburne gave his horse the rein,
and spurred onward. It was the first time he had
passed the fatal spot by night since his father's death.
The superstition of that period invested all such locali-
ties with gloom, and already had it been rumoured that
the spirit of Sir Charles had been seen there. No
wonder, then, that he held his horse with a firmer rein
as he approached the spot. He glanced around—suddenly the moon was darkened—chill overspread him.
The river was running peacefully, but gloom entered
into his soul, and he fancied he saw as in the picture
he had given to Sir Allan, the white hairs of his father
streaming in the blast. He was certain that he heard
an imploring voice cry, " Masses, Roger, for your soul

and mine—masses, masses, not gold!" Was he mistaken? We know not, but his horse needed not whip nor spur to add to the impetuous rate at which he galloped to his own stable door. The servants at Cunswick that night whispered one to another, as the groom described the foam and tremor of the steed, and the serving man hinted at the scowl and gloom on his master's brow.

    *   *   *   *   *   *

It was Shrovetide, and saint and sinner having been alike shrived by the grace of the Virgin Mary and all the saints, through the mediation of Holy Mother Church—the usual festivites commenced. The great day, however, was the Tuesday, on which the noble owners of Kendal Castle took part in the enjoyment, and invited the presence of all the neighbouring families. The auspicious morn had risen, and crowds of visitors flocked into the town. Soon the different hostels were crowded, and horses were tied in all quarters where they could obtain standing and provender. The scene of enjoyment was an open green at the foot of the hill on which the castle stands, immemorial usage having confirmed it as the place for the games of the people. Bright coloured booths and pavilions encircled the ground, the principal of which stood on the south side, appropriated to the use of Sir Thomas Parr, his family and guests, with an elevated gallery for the ladies.

Soon after eight o'clock, the occupants of this space were numerous, each engaged in observing the arrival of fresh comers. Prominent among the rest were Walter Strickland and his bride, the fair heiress of the house of Conishead; the Thornboroughs of Selside Hall, the Gilpins of Kentmere, the Mattinsons of Sleddale Hall. Leyburne, of Cunswick, arrived on a noble

charger caparisoned with richly gilt housings. His
own attire was in accordance, and his large, but far
from handsome, figure was prominent amid the crowd.
His dark eye wandered from object to object, and his
black plume seemed to cast a shade over a brow which
the scene ought to have made joyous. The party
from the Castle followed, preceded by heralds, proclaiming Parr the Lord of the Barony and President
of the field.

Shortly afterwards a modest palfrey, led by an attendant, bore Helen Bellingham to the ground. Her
kirtle was of green velvet, and a mantle of tartan enveloped her breast. Her cap was of gilt net work,
over which gracefully depended a rich veil of Flanders
lace. Young flowers of spring were formed into a gar-
land around her horse's neck, the gift of her cousin
Reginald Duckett, who had been on a visit at Burneside for a few days, and who rode side by side with
Sir Allan Bellingham, immediately after Helen. Few
personages attracted more attention than Reginald and
his uncle—the one in the youth of manhood, and the
other in autumnal vigour. The elder was mounted on
a large black horse of the description accustomed to
carry the weight of a man in armour. He was clad in
the manner of the north country, but bearing every
characteristic of the handsome gentility of middle age.
Reginald rode a grey horse of lighter make, a mixture
of Arab and British, such as were chosen in that day
by the knights accustomed to the chase and the tourna-
ment. His garments were of plain brown cloth, with
gold buttons, while the white ostrich feather which
shaded his cap, fastened by a clasp of brilliants on a
band of gold cloth, bespoke his gentle birth. Almost
last in the field came Godfrey, in the attire of an archer.
The crowd present prevented his reaching the ground

on horseback. He crossed the narrow wooden bridge which connected the field with the town. He had to dismount near the corn and fulling mill whose roofs were clustered with spectators, and thence to make the best of his way on foot through the crowd.

The bugles had sounded attention, and the heralds proclaimed the programme of the games. Jousting at a board elevated on a pole was first practised, and here amid the mass of competitors, Reginald excelled. As he received the chain of merit from Alice Parr, and with it a smile from Helen Bellingham, Leyburne's glance was one of vindictiveness. He, too, had striven hard for the prize, but the Lord of Grayrigg had left him far behind.

Throwing the bar, the quoit, and the spear, wrestling and foot races, followed, in which the nobler heroes of the field took part. Last and the chiefest came the archery. Here all were at liberty to compete. A chosen party of Kendal bowmen had united under Godfrey Bellingham, and challenged all comers. On the herald proclaiming their defiance, the troop marched to the front of the Baronial stand, and in excellent chorus, amid the cheers of the auditors, adopted the following song, being one of the many which associated the Kendal archer with every excellence in his profession.

In field or in foray, in salley or siege,
We ever are ready to fight for our liege.
Our bows are well tempered, our shoulders are strong,
Our arrows keen pointed, well feathered, and long.
In the rattle of battle, how dreadful the sheen
Which flashes from shafts shot by archers in green.

The stag of the mountain sees huntsmen afar,
He snuffeth the heath-blast nor careth for scar.
He heareth the horn and halloo of the hounds,
And gallantly over his rock path he bounds.
But mark, now, his bearing—for, lo! he hath seen
The bonnet and plume of an archer in green.

His footing now fails him, the tear in his eye,
Tells a sad tale of sorrow—he knows he must die.
He falters, he fails, lo! he faints on the ground,
For the eagle-winged arrow hath well'd from its wound.
For virtue and valour, for manhood and mien,
There never were archers like those clad in green.

Let the footsteps of foemen be heard in our land,
The knight takes his charger, the horseman his brand,
The servant his halberd,—but victory frowns,
Till forward come archers who win her bright crowns;
Then she twines her gay laurel leaves, worthy a queen,
Round the pledges of love—fixed in bonnets of green. ·

SECOND EPOCH.—PART II.

The song had not died away ere a crowd rushed forward to accept the challenge. The targets were prepared; the arrows flew with a truth to their aim which
elicited shouts of applause even at that age. The
number of competitors gradually diminished, as each
vanquished bowman withdrew from the conflict. The
distance of the target was gradually lengthened,—and
at last Godfrey, Thornborough, Reginald, and Leyburne were the remaining rivals. The interest of the
assembly was now intense. As each arrow winged its
way, the silence was deathlike, and as it struck the
target, a shout like the sound of many waters ascended
to the sky. Reginald and Thornborough were vanquished. Again the distance was re-measured, and
Godfrey and Leyburne were the sole competitors. How
carefully each then examined his bow, how narrowly
did he prove his shaft. Godfrey's arrow, amid the
tempest of applause, pierced the very centre of the target, with a ringing sound which betokened its force.
Leyburne followed. Breathless expectation awaited
the result. To mend the aim seemed impossible.

No! Roger's shaft struck the arrow standing in the target, and split it in twain. The old castle echoed the shouts of the spectators, which were reverberated by the rocks of Kendal Fell, and the bowman saw that Helen was pleased. He was delighted—felt that he must now win the day, for Godfrey had shot his last arrow. What was to be done? The judges awarded a fresh trial. Roger offered his quiver to his rival. It was not at hand; at last a retainer brought it forward, and presented a shaft to his master. Roger, with a careless air, handed the rest to Bellingham. His arm wavered slightly, but the arrow obeyed the practised eye, and pierced the target. Godfrey was now confident—every arrow that he had sped had been nearer the bull's eye than the one flown before. Straight started the shaft for the goal; the bowstring rung music to his brother archers, and a murmur of triumph was heard, when the arrow scintillated, diverged, and fell short of the mark. The feather had been loosened, and, like the rudder of a ship, had misguided the arrow's course. The murmur of triumph was turned to one of dissatisfaction, and the mutter of "dishonourable malice" overspread the field. The judges had, however, decreed that the trial was over. Leyburne received the prize from Alice Parr, who gave it heedlessly, and he could detect no smile on Helen's lip. The thought of vengeance pierced his soul.

The invited guests retired to the castle, in whose lofty hall they enjoyed the hospitality of their worthy host. Gaiety should have been there, but it was half repressed. Yet few were happier than Godfrey—his feelings were not easily disturbed. Helen was bantered with her early prospect of giving a similar entertainment, as mistress of Cunswick. Reginald heard it —pitied his cousin, but there was no chance of avert-

ing the engagement—and, notwithstanding his increased dislike of Leyburne, he himself had no intention of interfering with the contest. Still, as he
watched her light-heartedness and Leyburne's brooding brow, he mourned over the decree that was about
to give so tender a lamb to the protection of the
wolf.

When the company had dispersed, Reginald rode
leisurely home, attended by a single servant. The
midnight bell had tolled. It was dark, but his horse
took the well-known path fearlessly, and Reginald,
unheeding the reins, was buried in contemplation.
Presently he heard the tramp of horses' feet rapidly
approaching. " 'Tis only the drunken peasants hastening homewards," he muttered to himself. The
shriek of his attendant, and the start of his own horse,
however, made him, a moment after, instinctively draw
sword, and immediately three horsemen were around
him. Two conducted the attack, while the third held
aloof, watching the event. Skilled in the science of
defence, Reginald speedily wounded one, and his sword
had drunk the life-blood of the other, when the third,
with the ferocity of rage, attacked him with adroitness
and force. 'Twas an equal contest, but the arm of
Duckett began to fail, and he would soon have fallen,
had not the sound of voices been heard. The assailant
turned his horse and disappeared, but not until Reginald's sword had pierced his side, which, on wheeling
round, had been exposed, unguarded to attack. When
the parties, whose voices had dismayed the assailants,
appearing, Reginald was grieved to find his own attendant slain. One assassin lay dead on the ground,
the other was missing. Morning, however, found him
at a short distance, having expired from his wounds.
Who was he who had escaped? The night was too

dark for Reginald to answer this. Besides, he had also been severely wounded, and delirium had rendered him utterly unconscious of what had occurred. Strange to say, Leyburne had also been attacked on his way home from the Castle, and narrowly escaped with his life. He gave a particular description of the villains who assailed him, and the road where it had occurred was sodden with blood, but no discovery could be made. The dead bodies of the men who assailed Duckett were hung on gibbets on Castlehow Hill. Numbers crowded to see them. A few recognised them as individuals who supported themselves among the hills by killing game, or helping themselves, where they could do it safely, to the domestic game around the barns of the yeomanry. They had been observed amidst the crowds attending the sports, but no other information could be elicited. Time sped on. Sir Allan had paid many visits to Reginald, who was fast recovering. Sometimes Helen accompanied her father, and the attendants ever said her visits were better medicine. Godfrey was Leyburne's visitor, whose wounds had festered, and were still in an unhealthy state. Deep mystery still veiled the assassins.

By Whitsuntide, Reginald had been able to get over to Burneside Hall a few times, when he expressed to Sir Allan his intention to visit his old friend Walter Strickland, whose kind attentions he had experienced in his illness. The considerate uncle, unwilling as yet to let him take the ride alone, volunteered his company. From Grayrigg Hall they skirted the common of Hay Fell to its end, passed down by the then sequestered habitation of Natland Hall, forward to where a narrow arch spanned the Kent. Reginald had never seen the spot since childhood, and as his spirited horse could hardly be persuaded to cross the unbuttressed bridge, he dismounted, while the groom led it over. Duckett had seen the beauties of foreign lands. It might be that a sick chamber doubly enhances the loveliness of scenery—it might be that he loved, with filial love, his native vale, but certainly he then thought that no scene more striking had ever met his view. Below the bridge, the trees in a wood hung their shadowy branches over the stream, which moved stilly and black as Tartarus, in the narrow channel which it had hewn for itself out of the limestone rock. It was the personification of gloom. Above, the river came rolling on playfully, until it dashed itself in a cataract, and all its youthful vigour was coffined in the death-like darkness below the arch.

Reginald was rivetted with the scene; he crossed the bridge, and, to see it more perfectly, ascended the western bank. He had not gone far when he was attracted by a natural cavern in the rock, into which the water flowed in flood time. He looked into the opening at the top, and was startled at the sight of a human form, apparently lifeless. It was the body of a man advanced in life, but without a symptom of decay. His exclamation of surprise called around him Sir Allan and his attendants.

" Praise to the Blessed Virgin !" exclaimed Bellingham.

" Who could have thought that my hands should ever again have smoothed the brow of the friend of my boyhood, or placed the sign of the cross on the threshold of Cunswick Hall."

It was the body of Sir Charles Leyburne. Marvellous to relate (as if to fulfil the prediction that foretold that he would be laid in the tomb of his fathers), time had produced no change.

Directions were given to have the corpse properly

carried to Burneside Hall, as it was deemed inexpedient in Roger's state of health, suddenly to inform him of the body's being found.

Much to Helen's discomfort, Godfrey, his father and Duckett, would not obey her summons that evening to supper. They were in their council chamber.

"I cannot, I won't believe it," uttered Godfrey.

"Would to heaven it were not so," added his father.

"I concur with you, sir, in that wish," replied Reginald, "but I fear the testimony is too good to be disputed."

"We will see for ourselves," said Godfrey, and started up.

Lights were provided, and they proceeded into the chamber, where in feudal state the body of the deceased lay. Sir Allan wept, as the light glancing on the face imparted a smile to the countenance of his deceased friend. He was roused, however, by Rupert's cry,—

"May the curse of Cain light upon him!"

The cloth had been withdrawn from the right breast of the dead, and there was the wound of a poniard.

"Caution," said Reginald, "'tis a fearful thing to charge the murder of a father on his son; perhaps the wound may have been produced in the course of the body down the river;——but I see your father can bear the scene no longer; let us retire, and after supper concert suitable measures."

Leyburne's wounds had not improved under the care of the leech who attended him. His agitated and disappointed feelings at the postponement of his marriage with Helen were increasing his fever, and preventing his recovery. Father Leonard, the priest of All-Hallow's Chapel, had been to see him, and had appointed a time for confession more than once, but Roger had always been unusually ill. His servants were beginning to be anxious about him, and his incoherent expressions had frequently startled them. One old man who had sat up to be ready at his call, had been alarmed with conversation going forward at night, when no visitor was present. The other attendants disbelieved it, but the old man held to his tale.

'Twas the day after the late conversation at Burneside Hall, that Bellingham and Duckett proceeded to visit Roger, to announce the finding of his father's body. They were shown into his room; it was a large oak wains-coated apartment. The narrow windows, shaded by a purple damask curtain, added to the gloom; so that at first they could scarcely distinguish the invalid.

He lay on an ancient oaken bedstead, hung with crimson Louvaine cloth. Its many posts stood on the floor apart from the bed, at whose head the shield of the Leyburnes was carved and emblazoned. Roger received them with apparent warmth, but care marked his countenance.

On learning the discovery of the body, he asked, " Did the finders commit it in its putrified state again to the river ?" and his features expressed dismay when he learned that his supposition was incorrect. At last Sir Allan informed him of the wound on the breast. Leyburne expressed surprise, and immediately asked when they proposed to entomb the corpse. Bellingham replied that it ill became the honour of the family to have a hurried funeral—and that the body ought to remain in state for visitors to see, and for the priests to come and say masses over it.

When Roger heard the word " mass," his face became livid, his hands grasped each other, he uttered some incoherent expressions, and at last called loudly —" A priest for my soul, for my soul." A messenger was immediately despatched for Father Leonard ; a few minutes saw him returned, with a solemn-looking stranger monk, whom he had met coming on the very errand of seeing Roger. The stranger was tall and of striking figure. The rigidity of his features expressed severe penance. His deeply-furrowed brow overhung coal-black and brilliant eyes. Age was not expressed in his projecting eye-brows, nor in the long and sable beard which descended to his girdle.

He saluted Roger on entering. "Well son," a "concern for thy soul has brought me far to see thee."

"Welcome, father," replied the suffering man.

"Sirs," said the monk, addressing Bellingham and Reginald, "our interview with our dying son is sacred."

They were about to retire, when Leyburne, raising himself with unusual energy in his bed, exclaimed, with looks of haggard despair and derision :—

"Let them abide here, father; I will tell them all. Aye, go you Duckett to her who loves you—I know she loves you ;—how she smiled on you at Shrovetide, although her faith was plighted to another ! Go and tell her that to win her I have condemned my soul."

The monk's brow seemed to flash with a smile—it was momentary.

"Yes," proceeded the now almost frantic Leyburne, "I see it now—his white hair in the darkness of night, —and I hear now the old man as he cried, ' Roger, am I not your father ?'—but the gold, the price of her hand, was dearer than my father ;—the gold—yes, the gold. His body is found did they say ?—with the stamp of my dagger in his heart ! Tell her all ; and let the curse of a dying man rest——No ! no ! I cannot curse her——rest on his own soul," muttered the poor wretch, as he sank exhausted on his bed.

The monk turned to Sir Allen and his companion with a glance and a sternness that made them start.

"Ye have heard the confession of our son. I must now apply the awful rites which the dying may share."

"Not yet," exclaimed Leyburne, arousing from his death-like exhaustion,—"Reginald, it was I that bribed thy assassins, and wounded thyself. Would that thy life's blood had escaped from the gash! But thy arm was too strong, and my blood needed no new assailant to ensanguine the ground where I was said to be attacked. Oh! that even now I could reach thee"—and he clutched a dagger from the head of the bed, and struck the air in the direction where Duckett sat.

He was exhausted. Sir Allan and Duckett needed but a look from the monk, and they retired. Both were petrified.

Loud words were heard from Roger's room soon after they left. "Not yet—not yet," were uttered in piercing tones—then all was still.

Long they sat, for the exit or summons of the monk. Death-like silence pervaded the house. The evening closed in. At last Gilpin, who was in attendance upon his lord, exclaimed, "By my faith, the monk and the sinner will want a light."

He seized a lamp, and knocked at the door; there was no answer, though the knock was thrice repeated. The others had gathered around him; he burst it open—a blue flame seemed for a moment to encircle them all. It illumined the apartment, and they saw Leyburne lying dead on his bed, his own hand holding the dagger which still remained in his side. The contortions of his face were horrible,

But the monk—who was he? All looked around, but in vain. A cold chill crept over the group. Only Sir

Allan whispered to himself, " Aye," he said, " never will I be over-reached even by a cowl-covered head."

We need not describe how Sir Charles was buried with honours at Wensleydale; nor how the cursed bones of his son whitened the wild scar, and how his ghost visited the ledge of rocks that overhung Cunswick Hall.

Neither need we detail the prayers which ascended from Helen to the blessed Virgin, whom she continued to thank for her deliverance from the grasp of the wolf, —until she began fervently to beseech a blessing on her now almost constant visitor, the noble-minded Sir Reginald.

NOTE.—The place of Sir Charles Leyburne's murder is called " Carlan Steps" to this day.

I

BERNARD GILPIN, OF KENTMERE HALL.

" Enquire I pray thee of the former age, and prepare thy-self to the search of their fathers : . . . shall not they teach thee, and tell thee, and utter words out of their heart ?"——Job, viii. 8, 10.

INTRODUCTION.

I had been conning over the lights and shadows of Papal History ; and had derived much both of plea-sure and instruction from my speculation—such in-struction and delight as always accompany our con-templation of a masterly painting, filled with charac-ters and costume which we are satisfied had once an existence in all their pompous and picturesque reality, but which, while we gaze, recal forcibly to our minds the despotic and lawless power and passions amid which these realities had their being and sustenance, and which at the same time arouse within us a con-sciousness of security and a feeling of thankfulness that this antiquary-beloved state of things has passed away for ever, and that notwithstanding the many dis-parities which still exist, the general condition of man-kind has been materially benefitted by the change.

History—thus ran my cogitations—History with a consideration to the advancement of social happiness, possesses more than the fascinations of romance. Our conviction of the truth of what we read gives it all the value, without imposing upon us the humiliation inflicted by a formal moral lesson. The knowledge that we are unravelling the clue of that strange labyrinth through which humanity has struggled to its present stage, fully supplies the place of imagery, and not only rivets our attention, but fills us with emotion and awe.

With what sensations of humbled vanity and subdued selfishness do we muse and marvel over the instructive secrets which History, beyond all other booklore, has to disclose. The strength and the weakness of heart, the majesty and littleness of mind,—the contradictions and utter inexplicability of character that pervade or constitute mankind, laid bare and exposed as they are in every teeming page, if they do not make us more in love with our fellows, at least render us more tolerant and charitable towards the frailties and errors of one another. Nor is this all. Our nature becomes purified by the knowledge we attain of the insufficiency or worthlessness of vain pursuits. The toils, the anxieties, the meannesses of ambition, contrasted with their humiliating results—satiety, disappointment, misanthropy or despair—pass in review before us with the convincing vividness of experience. We cannot in the closet be dazzled or misled by the *ignis fatuii* of greatness or glory,—whose rays indeed seldom extend beyond the circumscribed circle of the passing pageant ; but—the praise and envy, and malignity of contemporaries having ceased to bias our judgment,—the Standard substituted is that of wisdom, virtue, and utility, which are the sole tests of Fame ; and whatsoever reputation shrinks from these tests, can boast of nothing better or higher than notoriety.

History teaches us to examine our capabilities as
well as our impulses. It dissipates our unctious notions that there may come on earth a reign of universal
peace and happiness; but, while it convinces us that
life in every stage and rank is only a scene of probation and endurance, it imparts to us the salutary knowledge that half our misery is of our gratuitous making.
The evils of our existence, which we are so fain to shift
from our own shoulders, and attribute to the errors of
government, the injustice of society, or the aberrations
of Fate, are too often the effects of our own want of
energy or perseverance, of our insatiable love of change,
our constitutional dissatisfaction, or the perverseness,
envy, or uncharitableness of our hearts. Were proper
scrutiny applied to our dispositions—our capacities for
perfectibility,—were we to institute comparisons between ourselves and those who have gone before us,
and left their lives a study to mankind, we should root
"the old woman" from our fevered bosoms, and
arise from our studies, better, wiser, and more contented beings.

And History is not destitute either of those other
and more universal attractions which seduce persons to
squander their susceptibilities on fiction and romance.
There are quiet nooks in History, recalling all that was
best of our youthful lives and affections,—all that our
manhood's hopes and wishes tend to ;—scenes redolent
of beauty and joy and peace and tenderness,—with
pleasant faces looking out upon us in our researches,
such as we feel we already love and long to be familiar
with hereafter. And then, too, there glide before us
visions of stern and dark and haughty visages,—souls
scathed and fiery, tossed by tempestuous passions, or
maddened with the excitements or remorse of crime.
The Drama is not more replete with gorgeous illu-

sions, than is History with the varied characters and incidents which makes us read and pause, resume and wonder.

And the History I had been reading—that strangest of all the strange chapters in the annals of humanity! The terrible reality of the boldly limned, picture wrought as it was of the apparently dissonant elements of power and imbecility, magnificence and abjectness, meekness and pride, generous devotedness and superstitious cruelty, which at all periods, and in all countries, have, more or less, distinguished the Catholic hierarchy, and yet allowed it to acquire and maintain an almost superhuman influence over men's minds—had impressed me with a kind of haunted feeling, such as occasionally remains with and overcomes us, after a dream, which, notwithstanding our reason and manhood, we can scarcely avoid regarding as ominous of some impending danger. There is a degree of mystery and awe, a something more subtle and spiritualized than belongs to mere worldly considerations connected with almost every event in the rise and progress of Christianity; and more especially with regard to the Church of Rome;—that link, which, however we may deprecate its abuses or deplore its errors, seems still to bind us to the apostolic age, and thus to preserve unbroken a chain of communication with divinity itself. With all that legislation or reformation has effected, we cannot help occasionally looking back upon the "scarlet lady of Babylon," our mother, as upon a giantess—wounded and maimed and prostrate indeed, but not mortally wounded—in the struggle to maintain her ancient authority over us; and as one who is in a condition not too hopeless to admit a probability of renewing, at some future day, her ancient struggle to our discomfiture. We need only turn to the schism which

within the last two or three years has arisen among
the legally constituted authorities of the church of
England, concerning the revival of obsolete observances, for a confirmation of the existence of such a
possibility; and this is supported by our statute-book,
through the lapse of three hundred years. Exclu-
sions, specialities, and abjurations of divers kinds,
have been and are resorted to, instead of reason and
conviction, to suppress and keep down the indomitable
spirit and perseverance of the adherents of Papacy;
and yet Papacy has nowhere been extinguished; but
has continued and will continue for ages to supply
abundant springs both of religious and political action.

I had taken up the volume which led to these reflections with a desire to discover the well-head, and to
trace, as distinctly as I might, the noteless streams
which after many wanderings and windings, after
overleaping the barriers and obstacles by which their
course and progress were in every direction opposed,
united at a point, and formed the great torrent of the
Reformation.

It was evening. The sun had gone down, and twilight was deepening over the neighbouring hills—discernible from the window at which I was sitting—ere
I had ceased to read; but at length the gathering dusk
had rendered the tracing of words an operation of
pain, and I laid down my book. The moon had already risen, pale and lustreless, as she always appears
when rising early on a winter's evening, over the pure
white crests of the snow-crowned mountains. But
gradually she grew brighter and brighter, and as the
stars, her dazzling hand-maidens, " man's heavenly
friends," sprang forth rapidly, one after another, to
cheer her with their brightness and beauty, I needed
no other than the soft light which gleamed through

my casement. More would have disturbed me, and
been out of character with my musings, which were of
a sober, dim, and monastic hue, like the events over
which I had been poring. My mood was that of a
waking dream or reverie, in which at first the present
and the past were indistinctly blended; but by degrees,
as the familiar things of everyday life, by which I was
surrounded, faded from my corporeal vision, the scenes
of bygone ages grew more vivid and impressive before
my mind's eye. The distant hills—bathed in the clear
moonlight, and standing out in relief against the grey,
monotonous wintry sky, assumed the forms of ancient
abbeys and cathedrals—their sharp peaks or broader
summits answering for pinnacles and turrets, and their
lower masses—here catching a faint ray of light, and
there enveloped in impenetrable shadow—correspond-
ing with cloisters and buttresses; with nave and aisles,
and chantries and chapels.

Thus my existence was thrown back, as it were, for
a space, into the days of feudalism; and I lived among
the men whose names have been sounded through the
world as those of saints and martyrs, heroes, and champions; or scourges, heretics, and fiends. I remained
upon the scene, however, an undazzled looker-on, without the slightest inclination to become a partisan. The
contests of the Reformers and Conservatives of old, like
those of the same classes in the present day, appeared
to partake too strongly of the fierce spirit of faction,
and to be influenced too greatly by personal prejudice
and predeliction to become otherwise attractive than to
the curiosity of a stranger. Accusation and recrimina-
tion, the magnifying of the petty interests of individuals
into matters of paramount importance to the kingdom;
the sophisms and fallacies of philosophers; the invec-
tives of priests, and the abject humiliation of the masses,

then—as now—were the staple of controversy. Before
ideas of self-aggrandisement, and party victory, every
other consideration was abased. Neither priest nor
layman was wholly untainted by barbarism and selfishness, or was free from the vices of avarice and ambition. Each was struggling for domination rather than
freedom ; and the questions of personal liberty and free
thought which gradually intermingled in the contest,
were superinduced upon the discussion, without having
originally formed part of it. The feudal nobles had
protected and defended the church against the tyranny
of royalty, until both priests and nobles had humbled
the power of the crown, and established for themselves
laws which restrained and controlled the sceptre ; but
the patronage of the military barons and knights was
scarcely less oppressive than the exactions of kings ;
and the clergy were compelled, after a renewal of strife,
to have recourse to the burgesses, and even to the
bondmen, to become their champions. This was the
beginning of democracy, not in England alone, but
throughout Europe.   .

It would be tedious to enumerate or describe the men
who passed in quick and fleeting review before me, with
mailed limbs, flashing swords, copes, mitres, sacerdotal
robes, and buff jerkins ; or the scenes which arose of
war and devastation, of cruelty and oppression, in which
the spear, the stake and faggot, the dungeon and the
gallows formed conspicuous objects. The question,
however, had arisen which neither persecution could
suppress, nor power smother — Should the mind and
creed of man be subject to the will of his fellow-man,
whatever his wealth or rank, under the order of things
which was crumbling into dust? Learning, science
and art, were developed in proportion as the people
emerged from the thraldom which had been inflicted

upon them by successive conquests; and they began
to be aware of their power and influence, from the stern
necessities for insurrection imposed upon them by the
despotism which sought still to retain them as serfs.

A period of confusion ensued—of passion and licence,
of civil war and party broil. In England the contests
of the white and the red rose had loosened the bonds
of the labourer, and stricken from the hand of the
aristocrat the fetters with which his humbler neighbours had been bound. The Parliament had arisen
superior to the crown, and a King—King Henry VII.
—had been appointed by parliamentary election—so at
least the Statute, which confirms his nomination,
avouches. When such had become the power of opinion
in matters of government, the church which had been
extending its power and wealth to a point of enormity
during the reign of terror, could not hope to escape
with its plunder, or retain its prerogatives. Wickliff,
though he had gone to his grave, and been nicknamed
a heretic after his death, had not preached unwisely or
in vain. He had sown the seeds of free thought, and,
with the restoration of order, these took root, and grew
and expanded, the lights of reformation arose one after
another to enlighten the prevailing mental and moral
darkness. Their growth was slow, it is true, but learning had hitherto been restricted to a class, and the de-
velopment of intellect must always more or less depend
upon contact with congenial intellect. Heresy, therefore, acquired to be a giant in its might, before it
avowed its faith or objects.

Among the number of those who were thus succes-
sively called before me, my mind recognised and attached itself to one individual, from whose life and actions
I gathered the history of the great change under which,
in the sixteenth century, the existing Church of Eng-

J

land sprung into being. It was BERNARD GILPIN, of
Kentmere, whose zeal, simplicity, unaffected piety, and
goodness of heart, gained for him among his contemporaries, and has embalmed for all time—the title of
THE NORTHERN APOSTLE.

CHAPTER I.

THE good seeds of Church Reformation in England
were sown prior to the reign of Richard the Second,
and the doctrines promulgated by John Ball, the
" hedge priest," as old Chroniclers contemptuously call
him, who officiated as chaplain to the enterprise of Wat
Tyler, for procuring the enfranchisement of the serfs
of the kingdom, were substantially the same doctrines
as were afterwards maintained by Martin Luther, John
Huss, Erasmus, Calvin, and John Knox—namely, that
faith could not be regulated by human law, that religious supremacy was human in its origin and institution,
and consequently not infallible, and that as the State
creed had been created by Statute, so it might and
ought to be destroyed. In the reign of Henry the
Fourth a long struggle took place between the Barons
and the wealthy Monastic orders, concerning the ap-
propriation of church property to alien priests—men
who not only did not preach to the people, but did not
understand the very language of the country from
which they derived their revenues, and never set foot
upon English soil—a contest which in the reign of
Henry the Fifth produced a dissolution and confiscation
of the property of the foreign priories and monasteries
throughout the realm. The reign of Henry the Sixth
was too turbulent to admit of much progress towards

Reformation of any kind; and the monarch himself was too superstitious, and too much the slave of his own confessors and chaplains, to desire that the work which had been commenced should go forward. He attributed, indeed, a part of his own misfortunes, and those of the nation, to the fancied wrongs which had been done by his predecessors to the Pope and the clergy ; and had he dared, he would willingly have receded. The reign of Edward the Fourth was alternately a stage of fierce strife, and degrading voluptuousness. The professors of religion as well as others were pampered or abased, according as they ministered to or opposed the power and pleasures of the king; and the consequence was that the religious orders generally sunk into the most abject state of mental and moral depravity. The picture which has been drawn by divines of their own age, who had more conscience than the mass, of their ignorance, indolence, sensuality, and hypocrisy, is too gross and revolting to be repeated in the present age. Under Edward the Fifth and Richard the Third, too little time was allowed for investigation or thought; but the talents of the latter, tyrant as he has been represented to us, were turned at once towards the subject of the public vices which revelled undisguised among the courtiers and nobles by whom he was surrounded on his accession ; and he made at once an effort to restore order and decorum. The prudent, cautious, and avaricious Henry the Seventh it was who first cast a longing eye upon the broad lands, and well-stored coffers of the priesthood ; and began to prepare the popular mind for the seizure which he meditated. Commissions and enquiries were sent forth in every direction to ascertain the mode of life and duties of the monks, nuns, and secular clergy ; with the injunction, more especially, to bring back a

true account of their incomes and benefices. Confiscation and forfeitures ensued—gradually indeed, and almost imperceptibly, except to the King's Treasurer—
whose hoards of gold and silver were greater at the
Monarch's death than had ever been amassed in the
vaults of the Royal Exchequer before ; and than ever
have been seen there since. Henry the Eighth had
originally been educated for the Church, and had in
his youth, perhaps, some prejudices in favour of the
profession he was to have followed ; but he loved plea-
sure, and the indulgence of his own will, better than
church or religion ; so that when his father's money
chests had been emptied, and no more could be raised
by direct taxation without driving the people to rebellion, he turned his eye towards the rich pastures in
which, had his brother Arthur lived and reigned, it
was intended that he should have fattened. In the
plenitude of his self-will and self-sufficiency he had
defended the Church against those who had attacked
it upon points of doctrine and observance. Here he
had found it invulnerable ; but its superabundant
wealth, while he was poor, offered an irresistible temptation to the sensualist. Arguments against any sect
marked out for plunder need never be wanting.
" Abominable lusts and vices" were discovered in pro-
fusion, by men paid specially to seek them out ; and
whose rewards appear to have been proportioned to the
enormities they severally brought to light. The nobility and wealthy commoners of the kingdom at first
marvelled in silence at this strange backsliding of the
" Faith's Defender," and then asked what it portended,
but, on being told that they were to share the booty
with the royal robber, they gave a ready assent to the
spoliation. The poor alone had nothing to gain by
the Reformation ; and the poor alone consequently

were the opponents of the measures of the Court—attracted by its new and *golden* light of "virtue, piety, and sound religion." In the year 1536, no less than three hundred and seventy-six abbeys, priories, monastries, and chantries were accordingly suppressed, and their possessions and effects of all kinds vested in the crown. It was a rich harvest, and satisfied all but the priesthood and the people. The latter, indeed, instead of being grateful for such excessive care for the health of their souls, broke out into open rebellion; and threatened a premature democratic revolution. They had been used to have recourse to the religious houses, instead of hospitals and workhouses—instead of soup-kitchens and infirmaries; and whatever excesses might have been discovered by strangers, deputed expressly to act as spies and informers, the humble neighbours of the monks had not been able to discover in the lives of their benefactors, the grievous errors and wickedness which had led to their being beggared at a blow—by Act of Parliament. Means, however, were found "to amuse the people by specious promises," and when they were appeased and had dispersed, six hundred and fifty three other monasteries were dissolved and appropriated. Thus the so-called Reformation proceeded year by year, till the end of the reign of Bloated Henry, the Tyrant.

The consequences were such as might have been foreseen. The rich livings which had been in possession of the monks who had appointed priests to perform the duties of the Church and administer the rites of religion, were now left without pastors. This is admitted in one of the Acts of Parliament passed in the first year of the reign of the boy King, Edward the Sixth, which states explicitly—"That many parish churches, through divers causes, were so much decay-

ed that their revenues and profits were not above the
clear yearly value of six and twenty shillings and
eight-pence, and were not a competent living for a good
curate ; yea, and no person would take the cure."
"The pretence," says a pamphlet of the period, believed to have been written by Latimer, Bishop of Worces-
ter, who afterwards suffered at the stake for his daring
heresy,—"the pretence for dissolving the religious
houses was to amend what was amiss in them. It was
far amiss that a great part of the lands which were
given to bring up learned men that might be preachers,
to keep hospitality and to give alms to the poor, should
be spent upon a few superstitious Monks, who gave not
forty pounds in alms, when they should have given two
hundred. It was amiss that Monks should have par-
sonages in their hands, and deal but the twelfth part
thereof to the poor, and preach but once a year to them
that paid the tithes of the parsonage. It was amiss
that they scarcely, among twenty, set one sufficient
Vicar to preach for the tithes that they received. But
see how what was amiss is amended, for all the goodly
pretence. It is amended even as the devil amended
his dame's leg, (as it is in the proverb),—when he
should have set it right, he brake it quite in pieces.
The Monks gave two little alms, and set unable persons many times in their benefices. But now where
twenty pounds were given yearly to the poor in more
than one hundred places in England, is not one meal's
meat given. This is a fair amendment. Where they
had always one or other Vicar that preached or hired
others to preach, now there is no Vicar at all. But
the farmer is Vicar and Parson altogether ; and an old
cast-away Monk or Friar, who can hardly say his
matins, is hired for twenty or thirty shillings a-year,
meat and drink,—yea, in some places for meat and drink

alone, without wages. I know, and not I alone, but
twenty thousand men know that more than five hundred
vicarages are thus well and gospelly served at this time
in England." The poor clergy, it is added, in an acknowledged sermon of Latimer's, being kept to sorry
pittances, were forced to put themselves into gentlemen's houses, and there serve as clerks of the kitchen,
surveyors, receivers or the like; or to follow some
trade or manual occupation in the character of publi-
cans, tailors, carpenters, or shoemakers; and many of
those who officiated as curates could scarcely read.

Such was the state of the Reformed Church of England when Bernard Gilpin began his ministry.

This great and good man was born at Kentmere
Hall, in the year 1517. He was the fourth son of Ed-
win Gilpin, of an ancient and honourable house, which
had been distinguished—according to Bishop Carleton,
his biographer, so early as the reign of King John, or
according to Dr. Burn, the Historian of Westmorland,
who has diligently traced the pedigree of the family—
in the reign of king Edward the Third, for public services. The fame of the race, however, began and ended with Bernard, so that it would be useless to raise
questions upon heraldic points concerning his gene-
alogy. It is enough that the position of his ancestors
was so far advantageous that it afforded him the means
of education and leisure for reflection, without which
he could have done little towards purifying the estab-
lishment to which he attached himself, or for the advancement of that pure religion of which he became the
most exemplary minister of his age.

It was to him an advantage of no small consequence
that he was born among the quiet hills of the North—
among the mountains, and lakes, and valleys, into
which the maddening excitements of faction, and the

influence of Court intrigue seldom penetrated. He had
been taught from childhood to look upon war as a
scourge to mankind. He had lost an uncle—William
Gilpin—in the battle of Bosworth Field, which gave to
England a new race of Sovereigns ; less fierce, it may
be, than the old Plantagenets, but not less determined
to maintain the power and prerogatives of the crown ;
and with dispositions to substitute money for blood in
extortion from their subjects. The country itself had
not sobered down entirely into peace from the long war
of succession ; but theoretical and speculative opinions
had taken the place of active strife and contention.
The Reformation of the Church—the power of parliament—the right of the people to personal freedom, and
of the nobles to maintain private feuds and armies of
vassals—were questions which were agitated in every
hall and homestead ; and awakened thoughts and reflections which had never before been discussed except
by the discontented and disloyal.

Bernard Gilpin, while yet a child, had begun to
think of these things. His mother—a gentle being—a
daughter of the house of Layton, of Dalemain—had
early inspired him with a love for the beauties of nature, and a reverence for the laws of nature's God,
which inculcated peace, the exercise of reason, humility,
mercy, and charity. He had wandered on the margin of the lakelet which meanders beside his native
spot—had climbed the mountains which overshadow
the hall in which he drew his first breath, and lisped
his earliest accents—had looked up to the sun and the
stars in their courses—had listened to the roundelay of
the rustic—shepherd and dalesman—and to the songs
of birds, and they had all harmonized with his aspirations for the dominion of universal love and harmony.
But when he turned to those who should have been the

promoters and teachers of peace and good will among men, he discovered one of the great errors of that and the succeeding age. The priests were not ministers of the Gospel; but professional preachers.

When less than six years old—a playful boy about his mother's knee—he gave indication of the strength of his perception and reason; and of that detestation of hypocrisy and mammon-worship which influenced his future life.

A wandering friar, in the thread-bare mantle of his order, begirt with cord and cross, and sandal-footed, appeared one Saturday evening at Kentmere Hall, to crave shelter and hospitality for the night. His garb alone—to omit all consideration of the universal hospitality of the age—ensured his welcome; and the seat of honour beside the blazing hearth was at once accorded to the reverend stranger. He was a man stricken in years, and the few locks that still lingered on his temples below the tonsure were white and venerable; but his quick and restless grey eye twinkled with mirth; and he had ever a jest or a merry tale upon his lips. Bernard, among the other inmates of his father's mansion, listened with wonder and delight to the strange stories and incidents of travel with which the holy father garnished his discourse; and beheld with no less astonishment the marvellous strength of his appetite and head, as his platter and cup were from time to time replenished at supper. The pious man was learned in the history of the court and the city—had lived in the camp, and been in lands beyond the sea, where a degree of pomp and splendour exceeding the marvels of fairy-land, as set forth in English song and legend, were maintained, both by priest and laymen; and on these he dwelt with a zest no other subject seemed to excite. If he spoke little of the precepts of Christianity, and the

K

miracles by which the will of God had been manifested
in the first ages, he dwelt with zeal and earnestness
upon the wealth which adorned the shrines of the saints,
the virtue of relics, and the power and state of the
Pope and Cardinals, in the city of St. Peter.   And still
he talked, and feasted, and drank till the sun had sunk
over the hills ; and still Bernard Gilpin sat on his low
stool beside his mother's knee, and listened and believed.   The good priest, however, was incapable of working a miracle to counteract the potency of the ale and
spiced sack which he consumed.   His accents gradually
came more trippingly from. his tongue, and his jests
were blended with snatches of song—at which the good
dame Gilpin held down her head, and the friar alone
laughed with glee.   Bernard remarked the change of
tone and manner of his instructor, and ceased to be edi-
fied by tales which he could not comprehend ; and on
being presently afterwards taken to his couch for the
night, he enquired the cause of the priest's aberrations.
It was a new idea—a subject for new reflection—to him
that a man should lose his reason, have his very powers
of speech paralysed, and utter falsehood as truth under
the influence of drink ; but he had learned that it was
so, and the lesson was not forgotten.

   The sabbath morn broke clear and calm upon the
lake and mountains, and the rays of the summer sun
glancing through the stained windows of the ancient
hall, glowed with rainbow hues like the plumes of
angels' wings.   Bernard Gilpin was up, and arrayed,
with the lark, and was basking in the sunlight, when
the friar, long before awakened, made his appearance,
with trembling hand, unsteady step, feverish lips, and
cheeks and eyes flushed and swollen.   The child, who
had been so inquisitive on the preceding eve, was now
moody, and made little response to the caresses which

were lavished on him; but took his breakfast and prepared for the religious service of the morning with more
of sullenness than was natural to one so young, so gay,
and so light-hearted.

"Gluttony, debauchery, drunkenness"—the special
vices of the day, were the burden of the friar's sermon
in the little manorial chapel. The man who uttered
the denunciations of heaven's wrath against those who
indulged in these vices, was unabashed and unmoved,
except by the vehemence of his own language and
gestures; but the most attentive of his auditors was a
child, and he wept.

"Why weep, my son?" said the mother of that
ruddy boy.

"Oh! mother," said Bernard, "Can I refrain from
grieving at the punishment this man has invoked on his
own head?"

Dame Gilpin pressed her kerchief to the mouth of her
child, and kissed his pale clear forehead.

CHAPTER II.

It need not be told again that the education of
Bernard Gilpin had commenced while he was yet an
infant. The lessons of his mother had sunk deeper
in his heart than the formal orations of schoolmen; and
Kentmere Hall was not without its library of missals
and chronicles, of sweet poetry, and scarcely less
poetical divinity. The priesthood, bad as many of its
members undoubtedly were, had great and honourable
names in its ranks; and these had wandered abroad
and preached to the feelings and reason of their fol-

lowers, and had left traces of their labours in every
quarter into which the soft and genial warmth of
christianity had penetrated. Bernard had learned
therefore both to think and to read; and ere he had
emerged from childhood, or was able to wind the bugle-
horn of his father—or to wield the heavy broadsword
of that father,—he was a marvel to the few cottagers
and mountaineers by whom the surrounding land and
vales were tenanted. He could tell them "like a book,
or a friar," of the saints and martyrs who had maintained the truths revealed by the prophets and evan-
gelists even to the death—could relate to them the
wonders performed by the old crusaders—by the kings
and barons and knights, who had half depopulated
England by their feuds; and could instruct them concerning the origin of border quarrels and family ani-
mosities, of which, though the effects of ill-will had
been transmitted through many generations of neighbouring chiefs, and remained still rife in the production
of evil passions, all other traces had perished and been
forgotten.

Thus Bernard was generally looked upon as destined for the priesthood, before he or those who had
power to dispose of him had thought of choosing the
path of his future life; and it was to this direction
from without, perchance, no less than to his native
piety, his studious habits, and his being a younger son
of a substantial, though by no means wealthy, house,
that the Church of England was indebted for its bright-
est and purest ornaments. He had long learned to
esteem himself as undergoing a noviciate for the ministry, and his parents had fostered his prepossession for
that pursuit, till he fell into the bosom of the church,
as if he had been, religiously and specially, dedicated
to it from his birth.

His sisters—he had three—wept when their kind brother was parted from them to proceed to Oxford, the proudest of our universities; but far—far from the mountains and woodland of Kentmere; much farther than, in these good and safe roads—of steam and railways, can be easily calculated; seeing that we reckon distance rather by time and difficulties than by miles. Bernard was still a boy—he was only sixteen—and he might forget or grow estranged, among the crowd of students by whom he would in future be surrounded, from those who were nearest and dearest to him. It was wholly uncertain when or how seldom tidings of his welfare might reach his home; and it was equally uncertain where his future lot in the great world, on which he was about to enter, might be cast.

Bernard himself, though buoyed by hopes which he could not define, felt sad, and the tear stole from his blue eye and trickled down his cheek as he pressed the trembling hand of his mother, and marked the quivering of her lip and the gathering moisture on her eyelid. He had, however, a word of comfort—drawn from holy writ—for all who pressed around to share his farewell; and after many caresses, many promises respecting his future conduct, and many partings, he tore himself from the assembled group, mounted the pony that was to carry him to Kendal, and urged forward after his father, who had gone before towards the foot of the lake, and had already reached the road leading to Staveley. There was a fond look towards the square old tower in which he had so long been nestled in safety and in love, as he rounded the dipping corners of the hills where the Kent flows downward, over its rugged bed, towards the sea; and then the scene of home set upon him, like the glory of a summer Sabbath to the overladen peasant of the plains.

It would be tedious to relate the particulars of a
love journey, barren, as his was, of adventure. From
Kendal he and his father journeyed by easy stages, towards the place of their destination ; keeping company
as long as their road lay in the same direction, with
the caravan of pack-horses and carriers which at that
period was wont to start for London every week, except at the worst periods of winter, with the celebrated
woollen cloths for which Kendal and its neighbourhood were then, and for ages before, famous throughout England ; and when their diversity of route parted
the travellers, the Gilpins took the best accommoda-
tion which offered, and wended on, with other merchants, for bad characters were not scarce in those days,
towards the seat of learning whither they were bound,
and where they arrived about ten days after quitting
the Hall at Kentmere head.

The youth soon attracted notice at Queen's College,
by his assiduity, his studious and persevering habits,
and by the gravity and gentleness of his manners—so
different from the usual ruffling of young men eager
for attention and applause, for triumph and distinction.
He carried the palm from many competitors, but he
claimed no victory, and escaped the enmity and malignity of his fellows.   He was anxious only to learn,
and be convinced, and in turn to instruct and convince
others ; and as he could not be turned aside from the
pursuit of knowledge by the quibbles and disputation
upon frivolous points, and questions of verbal criticism
which then constituted the chief exercises of college
life, his mind grew more expanded and his brain
better stored than most of his contemporaries ; insomuch that as soon as he was technically entitled
to literary honours, he was removed from his own college to a better foundation—that of Christ Church—in

compliment to and as a reward for his attainments and industry.

We shall not seek to follow him minutely through this portion of his career. The great questions of King Henry the Eighth's necessities, and of his long-desired divorce from Queen Katherine of Aragon, had raised other and more important questions, concerning the reformation of the Church, than Henry himself had contemplated, when he sought to rid himself of Papal supremacy and a wife, and to clutch the revenues of the monastic establishments throughout his kingdom. The superstitions of Rome, with regard to her sacraments—her adoration of images, her traditions, her mysteries—veiled in a language, strange to those who sought a knowledge of the Divinity through his acknowledged word—had provoked the research of, and drawn from his cell the bold and acute Erasmus; and thought had begun to open the flood-gates of light, and to dispel many of the mere chimeras of prejudice and custom. The reformation, despite the oft-exerted authority of the crown to stay its progress, went forward and prospered—gaining proselytes among the good and the learned wherever the stirring opinions of Reformers could find fair access. And when Henry was taken to his account, the councillors of his young successor gave a new impulse to enquiry, and led, as free enquiry always must, to the detection, exposure, and denunciation of new errors and abuses.

Bernard Gilpin, bred as he had been among good and pious Catholics—a communicant of the Romish Church, and looking with reverence upon ordinances which, ere he was born, had the sanction of many ages and of many good men, was not among the first to renounce the tenets he had once held sacred. If he doubted in some things, he felt that he needed conviction of the

falsehood or fraud of others; and he was none of those
who might be disposed to forsake a creed because it
was old and tame; and embrace a new faith because of
its daring novelty. He examined for himself. He even
disputed with Peter Martyr publicly in defence of the
doctrines they had mutually held in youth; but new
facts being gradually unfolded to him he eventually
quitted the Mass-book of the ancient hierarchy for the
book of Common Prayer, as set forth by the ministers
of young Edward.

A period of danger ensued. King Edward died—the
Lady Jane Grey was stricken down at a blow, and
Queen Mary ascended the throne, a determined bigot,
resolved to quell the dissensions which had arisen in
the kingdom on matters of religion, and with a spirit
and energy which made light of all opposition to her
sovereign will. During the persecutions which followed,
Bernard Gilpin was absent upon the continent, visiting
in turn Mechlin, Antwerp, Ghent, Brussels, Louvain,
and other places, where those who had been active in
the reformation were then congregated as in a monastery—some merely to avoid the stake which had been
prepared for them in their own land, and others the
better to prepare for fulfilling their high mission of
promoting the growth of truth and sound christianity,
by study, meditation, and the agency of literature in
places remote from scenes of mental distraction and the
terrors of a domestic inquisition. Gilpin, however, had
not fled because of danger, approaching or impending—
he had been previously appointed to a living by his
maternal uncle—Cuthbert Tonstal, Bishop of Durham,
and had resigned this, on being requested by the same
relative to proceed to Germany or Paris, to superintend
the printing of some books of divinity which the Bishop
had composed; and which it was neither safe nor con-

venient for him to print in England, where opinions
were so dissonant, and presses and printers so scarce.
This had been towards the end of the reign of Edward;
and consequently before the protestant persecution had
commenced. At the beginning of the reign of Mary
indeed, Tonstal had sought to recall him to England,
for the purpose of conferring upon him promotion in
the Diocese over which the aged, but not very orthodox
or consistent prelate, still presided. Bernard hesitated
for some time—he was absent about three years—but
at length, before the death of Mary, or the fires of
Smithfield and elsewhere had been quenched, he determined to return to his native land, and to take part in
the fierce struggle then existing. It was in vain that
the risk he ran—the dangers he was certain to encounter
—the impolicy—the madness of the step he meditated,
were pointed out to him—and depicted in their most
fearful—most appalling colours. He saw that religion
—the cause he had espoused—was likely to suffer in the
absence of so many of its best defenders; and he resolved to brave all perils for the sake of performing
what he conceived to be his duty as a priest and a
christian.

With the prayers and blessings of many to whom he
had endeared himself during his long sojourn among
strangers, he embarked from France to enter upon a
career, as full of high and noble enterprise, and of ad-
venturous incident, as most of the narratives which we
read concerning the exploits of heroes of romance.
But we must not enter upon this relation at the close
of a chapter.

CHAPTER III.

After visiting once more his family and friends at Kentmere, and renewing his acquaintance with the scenes which had been endeared to him by early recollections, and by the affections of his childhood, Bernard Gilpin took leave again of those familiar haunts, to enter upon his dangerous ministry. The only protection on which he had now to rely against the enemies of truth who abounded in the kingdom during the troubled reign of Mary, was that of his divine master. Tonstal, his uncle, though willing to serve and, perhaps, to shield him, under ordinary circumstances, was unequal to the task of preserving his integrity unblemished against the allurements and menaces of power, in an age of almost universal corruption, and though no persecutor himself, he sometimes permitted persecution in order to screen himself from the accusation of favouring heresy. Feeling, however, that he was sustained from on high, Gilpin faltered not, but at once began, in his church of Easingdon, to preach to the congregation entrusted to his charge, the doctrine of Salvation, through repentance and faith. No reserve,—no traditions of papacy,—no mincing of the gospel to mould its tenets to the support of human institutions, marred his zeal or restrained his eloquence. He denounced the popular vices which had been pampered by the priesthood, because they were profitable,—refused to accept, or to allow those who came to him for absolution from sin or crime to profit by offerings at the altar by way of atonement for their misdeeds; and by such a stern and novel course, he naturally enough roused against himself all the wealthy and powerful of the laity, and nearly all the ecclesiastics, among whom tho fame of his doings and sayings was diffused.

"He is heretical," exclaimed one, who was desirous of wandering on in the beaten track, and making tho most of his profession.

"He is an enemy to the church," cried another, "a scandalizer of the clergy; and a teacher of the doctrines of the son of perdition. He must be cited before the tribunal of the bishop, and compelled to recant his errors, or he must die as a foe to religion."

From the storm that had thus gathered around him the good easy bishop found it easier to remove than to defend his nephew; he accordingly bestowed on him the rectory of Houghton-le-Spring, in lieu of the living of Easingdon, and warned him, when he entered upon it, that unless he pursued the course pursued by others, and conformed to the observances of those who sought their personal safety and comfort, he would "live and die a beggar." He failed, however, to convince his auditor that the duty of a priest was regulated by the conveniences and self-seekings of the worldly minded. Trials therefore awaited him in his new residence, and for these he prepared with the devotion of one who stakes his life upon his conduct, and holds an immortal, dearer than an earthly, reward.

The parish of Houghton was one of the most extensive in the north of England. It comprised fourteen villages, the entire population of which were in a condition of such semi-barbarous ignorance as we can at this day form a conception of only by comparing them with the inhabitants of our most remote mountains and glens, where tourists never venture, and high roads and regular communications are unknown. The christianity of these wilds was still mingled with the Pagan super-

stition which it ought to have supplanted; and the
strange tenets of Woden and Thor, of the Druidical
times, and of the days of the Fairy creed, and of witch-
craft, were as firmly impressed upon the minds of the
people as the history of our Lord's life and death for
the redemption of man. The high ceremonials of
papacy were more regarded than the essentials of faith;
and that preacher was most popular among his congregation who would dole forgiveness to them for the
lowest consideration in current coin. Of the strange,
wild state of the country, and the general barbarism of
the age, a tolerable notion may be formed from the
fact that at the time Bernard Gilpin entered upon his
ministry, the very proclamations of Henry the Eighth
and Edward the Sixth for a change in the form of
worship had not been heard of, even by many of the
northern clergy.

Gilpin at once became a marvel to his flock, who saw
in him for the first time a teacher of the tidings of
eternity, who disdained to profit by public vice and
immorality. They crowded about him as they had
never thronged to hear any pastor before. They listened to his words, and were awakened as from a dream
to new life.

"It is an apostle restored to us, after the lapse of
ages," said they, who had derived new consciousness,
and been elevated and reformed through the new sense
of responsibility thus imparted to them.

"Say, rather," replied the indolent priests, upon
whose character and conduct the life of the rector of
Houghton was a standing reproach, "he is a disciple
of antichrist, and a minister of dissension and heresy."

Again, the anger, and envy, and hatred of those who
sought to extinguish the light of free enquiry in the
human mind were excited against the bold teacher of

gospel truths; and articles of accusation were again prepared against him in the hope that he might be brought to the stake. And this time they sought to make surer work than formerly. Instead of citing the good priest before Tonstal of Durham, his impeachment was laid before the wily and remorseless Bonner, bishop of London, and Grand Inquisitor of England.

"The heretic," said this fierce zealot, on reading the charges against Gilpin, "shall expiate his errors in Smithfield, within a fortnight."

The news of his intended fate did not surprise Bernard. He had long been prepared for the worst, and when urged to flee in order to avert the doom already pronounced against him, he sternly refused, seeing that by so doing he should be in some sort denying his faith, and confessing the weakness and errors of his ministration.

"If it be proper that I be delivered from my enemies," he said, "and the enemies of truth, the God whom I have served —how inefficiently soever—is able, and will take his own means to deliver me. If not, my body will but form another torch to light the nation to a knowledge of the true creed."

"But," replied Airey, his faithful and favourite steward and almoner, "the means of escape are in your power; and David himself hesitated not to avail himself of more than one opportunity to avoid the wrath of Saul."

"The faith and ministry of David were not called in question, Will," replied the preacher, "or he would have braved the worst. He scrupled not to encounter a giant when the welfare of God's chosen people required an exertion of individual courage and endurance."

"A temporary concealment at least," rejoined Airey, "might be resorted to. You have friends

among the neighbouring dales to whom you might en-
trust your safety, without foregoing your accustomed
duties."

"I have long looked for this hour of trial, Will,"
said Gilpin, "and will not now shrink from it. Let,
therefore, my funeral garments be made ready, that
it may be seen at the stake that I have made due and
decent preparation for the crowning scene of my labours."

Airey argued no longer. He felt that the calmness
and strength of his master were derived from the
purity of his heart and mind, and from his firm trust
in the righteousness and Providence of the Almighty.

A long funeral gown was made for the expectant
martyr, who, during the few days of freedom that he
was permitted to enjoy between that period and the
date of his apprehension by Bonner, preached as usual
and dispensed his hospitality with his customary cheerfulness. The mournful gloom which rested on the
brows of his auditors, and the increased earnestness
with which they listened to his exhortations, alone indicated that anything was likely to interrupt the sere-
nity of that genial springtime of Christian piety and
benevolence.

When the messengers came to convey him to London, they had not far to seek. He was in the midst of
the school-house which he had himself erected and en-
dowed for the purpose of teaching the children of his
parishioners the knowledge of themselves and their
Creator. His pupils clung around him when they
learned that he was a prisoner, and many a bold heart
and sturdy hand was stirred to resist the authority of
his captors; but a word from the good priest silenced
and subdued all but their tears and lamentations,
which would not be restrained when they knew that he

whom they loved and revered as a father was to be torn
from them, to undergo an ignominious punishment, for
having been to them and others the instrument of so
much good. With the men and women of the villages
and hamlets through which the cortége passed, there
was more difficulty, however, than with the children.
The news of his arrest circulated with the rapidity of a
battle-call for the resistance of Border forayers ; and
crowds gathered by the road side, and implored permission from the prisoner to rescue him and destroy his
oppressors. The road was lined for miles with these
suppliants, thronging before and behind in such numbers, as occasionally to block the mountain passes, and
to render impassable the fords through which the procession must needs proceed on its way ; and sorely were
the agents of Bonner afraid, when they heard the deep
and bitter muttered curses of the multitude, breathed
alike against the bigot Queen and her hated agents of
persecution. It was in the firm and mild expostula-
tions of their victim alone that they were indebted for
their lives :—but this, instead of inspiring them with
feelings of gratitude and veneration, served but to in-
crease their hatred and their thirst for vengeance. To
possess such abounding love was worse than either
treason or heresy :—it added the malice of fear and
humiliation to the ordinary rancour of bigot zeal.

Scarcely, however, had the prisoner and his conduc-
tors reached the confines of Yorkshire ere an accident
put a stop for some days to their journey. Descending
a steep hill, the horse which Gilpin rode stumbled and
fell, and the rider being precipitated to the earth, was
taken up with a fractured leg. It was in vain that the
inquisitors vented imprecations upon both horse and
prisoner. Had they attempted to proceed, their victim
would, in all probability, have eluded the flames which

were prepared for him, by a premature death on the
road. They conveyed him therefore to the nearest
town, and procured assistance to set his broken limb.
They could not forbear taunting him, however, with
what had befallen, as an instance of the divine displea-
sure against his heresy, and a punishment in addition
to that which awaited him.

He merely replied, with forbearance and resignation,
"That nothing can happen to man but through the
permission of God, who does all things for the good of
his creatures."

"And your broken leg," said Leyton, a familiar and
panderer of Bonner, "that, of course, was meant for
your special benefit?"

"I do not doubt it."

"The stake in Smithfield, too, has been erected for
your good?"

"If God so wills it."

"You will be a brave martyr, my master," retorted
Leyton, "till you come to the pile of faggots. There,
however, I have seen some of your kidney quail, as the
curling smoke and flame have blackened their delicate
limbs."

"My trust," said Bernard, "is in Him who suffered
for the truth, and endured every indignity, in Judea.
He condescended to suffer for the sins of others. Why
should I flinch from a chastisement inflicted for my
own?"

"Hear him, and note down his words," said Leyton,
"he blasphemes."

The protection on which Gilpin had relied, however,
was not withdrawn from him. While awaiting to recover his strength sufficiently to pursue his journey,
the joyful news was spread through the kingdom, with
ringing of bells and lighting of bonfires, that Queen

Mary was dead, and that Elizabeth had been proclaimed amid the acclamations of a people rejoicing in their
deliverance.

When the intelligence was brought to the bedside of
Bernard Gilpin, the good pastor, raising himself on his
arm upon his couch, mildly rebuked his persecutors by
saying, " Did I not say that nothing could happen to
us, but what is intended for our good ?"

The inquisitors, one by one, slunk away from the
chamber of their rescued victim, until the good man
was left alone to thank Heaven for his deliverance, and
to meditate upon the future prospects of untrammelled
religion in England.

CHAPTER IV.

On his return to Houghton-le-Spring, after having
been rescued, as it were, from the very foot of the stake,
Bernard Gilpin was received wherever he came rather
as a victor returned from conquest, than as a poor
preacher, liberated from persecution. By Bernard
alone the matter was treated as one unworthy to be
considered a triumph. He had deemed it, as he deemed
almost every event of his life, an act of probation, in
which he had been sustained by Providence, not to
swell his pride, but to fill him with gratitude, and en-
due him with strength for new trials. He rejoiced,
therefore, only inasmuch as he had been enabled to
resist the strong temptation of betraying his trust;
and he renewed his labours at once, after reaching
home, with increased zeal and diligence.

M

The fame of Gilpin had necessarily spread far beyond the wild scene of his pastoral charge; and now
that a Queen, holding a different faith to her prede-
cessor—a faith, indeed, which was considered as the
very opposite of papacy—was upon the throne, surrounded by new Ministers, anxious to remodel all
things, and to forward the cause of Reform as far as it
could possibly be urged — without infringing the
Divine right prerogatives of Majesty—those who had
been the objects of persecution, of odium, or even of
suspicion, in the last reign—without any very discrim-
inating regard, in all cases, to respective merit, were
naturally selected as the recipients of royal favours
and rewards. Bernard was thus chosen by Lord Bur-
leigh, to whom he had become known during the reign
of Edward the Sixth, as one who deserved promotion.
The Bishop of Carlisle, among others had conscien-
tiously maintained his creed—notwithstanding that it
was derived from Rome—through evil as well as good
report, and in the midst of difficulty and danger, as
firmly and consistently as when the smiles of fortune
had cheered him as his professor. It was not the policy
of Elizabeth or her council to leave power or patronage
in the hands of men of this bold and independent
stamp. The faith of a bishop must necessarily be that
of the Sovereign for the time being; and they only,
who, like the Vicar of Bray, could accommodate their
consciences to every fleeting change of " the gospel
according to law," might entertain a reasonable hope
of holding their ministry longer than their doctrines
should continue to be fashionable, as those of the
Court. The learned prelate of Carlisle, as one of the
non-conforming clergy, was deprived of his mitre,
and the diocese was tendered to Bernard Gilpin, " because he was a North countryman, and had been en-

dangered on account of his stedfast adherence to the principles of the Reformed Church." But the offer was declined.

Gilpin had, in fact, attached himself to his flock and to his duties by ties which might not be easily sundered, and "the Northern Apostle" did right to reject "the bubble reputation" for the substantial and glorious wreath of fame.

Shortly after his rejection of the "throne" of Carlisle, the patience and fortitude of Father Bernard were again severely tested; not on this occasion by temptation to his own profit, but by wrong and outrage—and the opportunity—so difficult to withstand—of avenging himself upon his enemies. The earls of Northumberland and Westmorland, prompted by their zeal for the Catholic cause, which appeared to have become desperate, rose in arms for the purpose of obtaining freedom for the exercise of their religious rites, if not of restoring the supremacy of their worship. The outbreak was supported by the populace; for in most parts of the country the cause of papacy involved the rights of the poor, and had the entire sympathies of all classes, except those who had been really converted from the ancient errors. The time was one of trouble and commotion through the entire north. Castles, villages, and towns became a prey to enthusiastic rebels, who marched with banners displayed, bearing embroidered chalices, crosses, and even the image of our Saviour crucified. Barnard Castle surrendered, Durham was sacked, mass was chanted once more in the churches; and bigotry and ravage stalked through the country. The usual quiet and secluded parish of Houghton was not suffered to escape during the excitement and confusion; and there, the harvest being just over, the barns and granaries full, and the fields and meadows well stocked with the fat cattle of autumn, "what had been designed," to use the graphic language of an old historian, "to spread a winter's gladness through the country, was, in a few days, wasted by the remorseless rabble." What could one man do to arrest the progress of such calamities? Bernard Gilpin merely opposed remonstrance and prayer to outrage; but even that seems to have had its effect in staying the hand of rapine; for, beyond his immediate neighbourhood the people and their possessions were left unharmed by the malcontents. In the day of retribution, however, the voice of the good man was not uplifted in vain. The Earl of Sussex being sent with a strong army to quell the revolt, soon dispersed the enthusiasts, and Sir George Bowes, placed at the head of a Special Commission to try the offenders, acknowledged that what mercy he showed to delinquents—small as it was —was at the instance of the rector of Houghton, who had implored him to spare the people, "who, being exceedingly ignorant, had been seduced from their allegiance by idle stories, and led to believe that they had taken arms in behalf of the coerced Queen, as well as of their ancient privileges and the right of worshipping as their fathers had worshipped for generations."

To estimate aright the many benefits which flowed from the teaching of Gilpin, it may be necessary to revert to the state and customs of the country when he first entered upon his cure.

He had, in the first place, some difficulty in finding a person for his clerk, who was able to read—writing was out of the question. The Sunday was the principal market day of his parishioners, and the church porch, even during the hours of service, was the mart of itinerant pedlars and dealers; while at festival times, lords of misrule, boy-bishops, morris dancers and masquers were accustomed to enter the church with music, song and jest, to perform their mysterious mummeries in the presence of the whole congregation. On one occasion, it is reported that he sent word to a neighbouring village of his intention to preach there on a certain day set apart for a holiday; when, on presenting himself at the church doors, he found them locked, and after tarrying for half an hour, ascertained that it was Robin Hood's day—and that the whole parish had gone forth to gather garlands and perform their May-day sports. "I was fain, therefore," said Bernard, "to give place to Robin; and let the tidings of salvation wait for a more convenient season."

At another time, while journeying, as was his frequent custom, through the least accessible vales, and among the glens and mountains of the border land, having previously given notice of his intention to preach there, he found on his appearance at the homely church of Rothbury, that a crowd had collected, not so much to hear his doctrines, as to witness a tumult which was likely to ensue between two rival factions. An hereditary feud had subsisted between the inhabitants of Tynedale and of Redesdale, which nothing had been able to abate at former meetings but blood. They were now drawn up in array in the small church-yard, eyeing each other with the gloom of deadly hate and fury; but each maintaining profound silence. The church doors were opened, and the parties stationed themselves on different sides of the church, still facing each other, and ranged in order as prepared to make, or resist, an onset, on the slightest signal. All were armed with dirks, swords, and javelins; and ever and anon, at the pauses of the preacher's discourse, the weapons were clashed

in defiance. It was a strange, wild scene. The ani-
mosities of men, blended with a thirst for knowledge of
the way of life:—hostilities in the very sanctuary of
peace and mercy! As the clang of arms grew louder
from time to time, Gilpin found himself compelled to
notice the unseemly conduct of the parties ; who, rever-
encing his character, and impressed by his exhortations,
promised to abstain from violence at least till the
service was concluded. He resumed his sermon, in-
veighed against the savage feuds of barbarous ages, and
so strongly dwelt upon their mutual responsibilities,
and shewed the inestimable benefits of forbearance and
kindness, without the exercise of which, faith in
redemption could be but a name, that, in the end, the
chiefs on either side consented to abandon all thoughts
of hostility during his stay in the country, and to endeavour, in the meantime, to settle their differences
without recourse to any future appeal to arms.

It was about the same period also, and in the same
uncivilised tract that on going one Sunday to church,
he perceived a large concourse of persons gathered
around a yew-tree which stood beside the church porch.
A glove was hanging from a branch, and armed men
were standing near to watch it. The priest made
earnest enquiries concerning the meaning of what he
saw, and was informed by the sexton that the glove had
been placed there as a challenge to whoever should dare
to take it down.

"Give it me," said the preacher without hesitation.

"Not I, indeed," replied the sexton—"I dare not."

"I must have it nevertheless," rejoined Bernard; and
reaching it from the bough, he thrust it at once into
his bosom.

No one ventured to molest or question him; and the
service was concluded ere the matter was again alluded

to; when taking the signal of challenge from his vest and exhibiting it to his congregation, he exclaimed, " I hear that one among you hath hanged up this glove in token of defiance to his fellows, even at the threshold of the house of the Lord. Behold I have taken it down." The challengers, abashed, sought his council in the vestry room, on his descending from the pulpit, and promised to relinquish the rude custom which had given him offence.

So great was the esteem in which his piety, charity, and goodness were held that the very thieves of the borders—and the population were nearly all cattle-lifters, and out-laws by practice, if not so proclaimed by the Border Wardens—abstained from committing depredations upon his property.

CHAPTER V. — CONCLUSION.

WE hasten to close our narrative of the Life of the Northern Apostle, which has grown on our hands to a much greater length than we contemplated, and has consequently become proportionably tedious to our readers and ourselves.

The following, which has reference to the magnitude of his labours as a pastor, is from a letter of his own to a friend :—

"I am at present," he says, "much charged with business, or rather overcharged. I am first greatly burdened about seeing the lands made sure to the schools, which are not so yet, and are in great danger to be lost, if God should call me afore they are assured. Moreover, I have assigned to preach twelve sermons at other parishes, beside my own; and likewise am

earnestly looked for at a number of parishes in Northumberland, more than I can visit. Besides, I am
continually encumbered with many guests and acquaint-
ances, whom I may not well refuse. And often I am
called upon by many of my parishioners to set them at
one when they cannot agree. And every day I am
sore charged and troubled with many servants and
workfolks, which is no small trouble to me; for the
buildings and reparations in this wide house will never
have an end."

As an instance of the stern determination with which
his resolves were carried out, the following anecdote
has frequently been related :—Gilpin was sent for one
day by Barnes, bishop of Durham, who required him
to preach a visitation sermon on the following Sunday.
He begged to be excused, on account of being then
about to perform his usual journey to Tynedale and
Redesdale; but the bishop, instead of admitting his
apology, suspended him from preaching, for non-com-
pliance with his mandate. The bishop, however, unable
to justify himself for so harsh and hasty a step, subsequently sent for him ; and many of the clergy being
assembled at Chester-le-Street, the place of meeting,
he was ordered to preach before the conclave. He
stated that he had come wholly unprepared, and urged
that he was suspended. His suspension was forthwith
removed, and he eventually complied. Instead of a
courtly sermon, however, as was probably expected,
Gilpin, who knew of the abuses practised in the diocese,
the ecclesiastical jurisdiction of which was little better
than a plea for the sale of canonical indulgences, in-
veighed more especially against the vices of the clergy.

"God hath exalted you," he said to the prelate, "to
be the bishop of this diocese, and requireth an account
of your government thereof. A reformation of all those

matters which are amiss in this church, is expected at your hands. And now, lest perhaps, while it is apparent that so many enormities are committed everywhere, your lordship should make answer, that you had no notice of them given you, and that these things never came to your knowledge, behold I bring these things to your knowledge this day. Say not, then, that these crimes have been committed by the fault of others without your knowledge; for whatever either yourself shall do in person, or suffer through your connivance to be done by others, is wholly your own. Therefore, in the presence of God, his angels, and men, I pronounce you to be the author of all these evils: yea, and in that strict day of general account, I will be a witness to testify against you, that all these things have come to your knowledge by my means; and all these men shall bear witness thereof, who have heard me speak unto you this day."

This freedom alarmed every one. As Mr Gilpin went out of the church, his friends gathered round him, kindly reproaching him, with tears, for what he had done, and saying, that the bishop had now got that advantage over him which he had long sought after; and if he had injured him before without provocation, what would he do now, when so greatly exasperated? Mr Gilpin walked on, gently keeping them off with his hand, and assuring them that if his discourse should do the service he intended by it, he was regardless what the consequence might be to himself.

During that day nothing else was talked of. Every one commended what had been said, but was apprehensive for the speaker. Those about the bishop waited in silent expectation, to see his resentment break out.

After dinner Mr Gilpin went up to the bishop to pay his compliments to him, before he went home. " Sir,"

N

said the bishop, " I propose to wait upon you home myself." This he accordingly did; and as soon as Mr
Gilpin had carried him into a parlour, the bishop turned
suddenly round, and seizing him eagerly by the hand,
said, " Father Gilpin, I acknowledge you are fitter to
be the bishop of Durham than I am to be parson of
this church of yours. I ask forgiveness for past injuries. Forgive me, father. I know you have enemies;
but while I live bishop of Durham, be secure, none of
them shall cause you any further trouble."

About the beginning of February, 1583, Bernard
found that his end was approaching. He ordered himself to be raised in his bed; and his friends, acquaintance, and dependants to be called in. He first sent for
the poor, and beckoning them to his bed-side, he told
them, he found he was going out of the world; he
hoped they would be his witnesses at the great day
that he had endeavoured to do his duty among them ;
and he prayed God to remember them after he was
gone. He would not have them weep for him; if ever
he had told them anything good, he would have them
remember that in his stead. Above all things, he exhorted them to fear God, and keep his commandments;
telling them, if they would do this, they could never
be left comfortless.

He next ordered his scholars to be called in : to
them he likewise made a short speech, reminding them,
that this was their time, if they had any desire to
qualify themselves for being of use in the world; that
learning was well worth their attention, but virtue was
much more so.

He next exhorted his servants; and then sent for
several persons, who had not heretofore profited by his
advice according to his wishes, and upon whom he imagined his dying words might have a better effect. His

speech began to falter before he had finished his exhortations. The remaining hours of his life he spent
in prayer and broken conversations with some select
friends, mentioning often the consolations of Christianity—declaring they were the only true ones; that
nothing else could bring a man peace at the last. He
died upon the fourth of March, 1583, in the sixty-sixth
year of his age."

The following appropriate close to the biography of
this good man is extracted from the *Visits to Remarkable
Places*, published some time ago by Mr Wm. Howit:—

"The fame of Bernard Gilpin had, from my earliest
youth, been in my mind one of the most golden and
sunshiny fabrics, that are built of wonder, love, and
veneration, in the heart of childhood, by reading or by
story of what is great, and picturesque, and beautiful.
The idea which lived in my imagination of him, firm
and glowing as my imagination itself, was of a tall and
venerable old man, wandering over vast heaths and
moorlands with his Bible in his hand, ready to confront the marauder in his way, and awe him with a
word of heaven's truth; to sit down by the swift stream
of his northern valleys, and in language of peace and
affection, and divine hope, with the solitary fisherman,
till he forgot his angle, and let his line float idly on the
water, his thoughts having flown far into the regions
of paradise; to sit, too, by the wayside-well and the
village cross, and hear the troubles of weary wayfarers,
and then comfort and relieve them ; to enter farms and
cottages, and be recognised and received as the prophets
and apostles of old, with sighs and courtesies, and a
running to and fro to cover the table for his refreshment, and spread the news of his arrival. I see him
stand with his hand on the head of some lovely child
speaking to its companions on the village green, with

the bright eye and smiling countenance of a most
child-like benevolence, and blessing them all in his
heart. I see him too in the more solemn hours and
duties of his office and his life ; now sitting by the bed
of crime and of coming death, combating despair, and
teaching the affrighted wretch where only in the whole
gloomy hemisphere the eye of mercy glanced through
the clouds; now rebuking the fierce brawlers and
scorners of the savage haunts that he visited ; and now
from some antiquated pulpit, or steps of an ancient
grange, pouring over the wandering crowd the eloquence of the heart and the news of Heaven. Perhaps
the name—Apostle, gave no small vividness to those
ideas; and as years advanced, I learned to love his
memory, too, for the grandeur and fortitude of mind
which made him bold and faithful against those worldly influences, of whose seductive or daunting potency
a child has no conception."

THE STRAMONGATE BARGHAIST.

"I saw it as plainly as ever these eyes beheld the moon at Martinmas," exclaimed Michael Mason, as he rushed into the guard room, situated at the gate on the north side of what is now called Stramongate Bridge.

"What was it you saw, you loon? Surely the beast with two horns must have been encountered by your gaping eyes," said old Denzil Masterman, roused from his slumber by the hurried entrance of his coadjutor.

"'Twas the lady in white," answered the still trembling warder.

"Nay, now 'an it be that thou are yet bleached by this white lady, cheer thee up with this jack of good Kendal ale; and Denzil poured out into a leathern mug a stream of the sparkling beverage.

Michael seemed to imbibe fresh courage, but we trow it was more from the companionship of his fellows, than the liquor he had swallowed. By this time the third of the group had been awakened, and Maurice Bateman was urging Michael to describe what he had seen.

"Well," said Michael, "my watch having expired, I was coming back, and, passing that creaking sign of the Dun Horse, which hangs half way across the street, just by the narrow entry where old Giles Kemp used to dye and shear his cloth, when turning round at hearing what I thought to be a dog barking, I saw a beautiful lady, with a robe white as snow floating in the air, going down the passage. I followed. She seemed to sail over the ground, and before I could overtake her, at the Kent side, she vanished into air."

"And if I had been there," said Maurice, "my feet would as soon have followed the trail of a wolf, as have gone after such a vision. It is no' lucky, Michael. You may go to Father Leonard's chair as soon as you like, and mind and confess all your sins."

"Hold," said old Denzil, "you are foolish lads— you forget that it's time to take the round; and the men with the pack horses wanted calling at two o'clock. If we are too late for them, we shall lose our bottle of sack; and if I mistake not, neither of you, boys, will be out again to-night, without more courage than your own."

The two younger guards seemed loth to brave the blast or the barghaist, so the sturdy old Masterman added, " Well, it must e'en be that my grey beard is not so taking to ladies in white, as the down on the cheeks of you youngsters. Stay you here, therefore, and when I return, I will tell you a tale about this same damsel, which few know but myself."

Maurice and Michael thought Denzil long in return-ing. At last, however, he came, and having despatched the packmen's bottle of sack around the fire on the hearth, the old man, turning to Michael, said—

" I think you heard a dog barking, did you not?"

" Aye," replied Michael, " but I did not see one, only I fancied I spied a dark shadow following the lady's footsteps, from which came several times a hollow bark; and as she disappeared, there floated to me on the gust which followed, a dismal moan."

" 'Tis the very same," said Denzil ; " you have been favoured with what few have seen; and ill betide me if your sweetheart does not give you a hearty amen when you show her the wedding ring. But I promised you my tale, lads. My father was as good a soul as ever wore Westmorland grey. Poor man, he was eighty seven when he died, and but a short while before that event, he called me to his bedside, and said, ' Now Denzil, I have often thought I would give you a history of my life.' This he proceeded to do ; it was a most eventful one, and amongst other things he related the following :—

" I was for ten years a servant with old Sir Arthur Wilson ; he who lived in the Black-hall, Stricklandgate, as good a master as ever paid wages. The poor often blessed him, and his sweet daughter, Mistress Edith—sure there never was a better heart, or a bonnier eye, than she had. Often have I watched her helping the old man to walk. Even when his weight was fit to drag her down, he would have no other assistant. And she nursed him with as much care, as the hen nurses her young, and when his last hour came, she closed his eyes with her own hands.

" Alas, for her—the sod had not covered her father's bones, when her uncle Nicholas came down from the south, to act as executor, and shewed, by the will, that he was to have all the management. But there were those, nevertheless, who whispered that Father Gervase had mentioned on his death-bed (which took place just prior to the death of the old man) that Sir Arthur had wished the priest to make his will for him, and that in that will he had left all to his daughter,

with a proviso that if she should have no children, the
property should go to the Abbey at Shap. Nay, it was
said that some smouldering fragments of parchment
were found among the embers on the hearth in the
library at Black-hall, after the uncle came down, and
many thought that the now will produced by Nicholas
was, to say the best of it, unlike the old one. But be
that as it may, the poor young lady soon found out
that her uncle Wilson was not like her father, good
Sir Arthur. For he had not been long at Kendal,
when his son came to join him, as rough and wordly
a rogue as the country could breed. Nay, I doubt
whether he was even born in the fair County of Westmorland. He made love to Edith, but her gentle
spirit shunned such a roystering husband; and like
the fawn of the mountains, she fled from the idea of
contact with the young man. Her uncle was grieved;
and after much persuasion told her at last that she
must either make up her mind to marry her cousin
Mark, or be content to take the veil.

"Edith, of the twain, would gladly have preferred
the latter, but wherefore was she to be compelled?
She resolved to ask who had authority to force her to
sacrifice herself to Mark, or to embrace the alternative
of perpetual seclusion from society. The inquiry of
the simple-hearted girl was met with a frowning brow,
and an angry reply. Her uncle said that her father's
will enabled him to enforce the sacrifice he demanded,
and nothing but compliance would satisfy the obliga-
tion. Edith thought to herself how little her father
would have been pleased with Mark, and felt assured
that his will *must* have been falsified; but, alas! she
had no friend to consult with, or to guide her, and no
course but a compulsory one appeared open to her.
At length her uncle, wearied with her stupidity and

obstinacy, as he termed it, limited the lovely orphan to
a term of four weeks to decide, at the end of which she
was either to give her hand to his son, or to adopt the
austerities of a religious life.

Already was the month well nigh expired, and no
hope of deliverance or prospect of evading her fate appeared. One anchor only was left, namely, the inter-
position of the gallant Ralph Thornburgh. This noble
cavalier had followed the Clifford to the wars of Spain,
and ere his departure, with the sanction of her father,
Ralph and Edith had naturally pledged their troth before father Gervase, to be faithful unto death. On her
father's decease, Edith had written to Thornburgh, and
had been hourly expecting him,—or, at least a reply
from him, to avert, she knew not how, her threatened
fate. She dared not mention this to her uncle, as she
knew it would aggravate his wrath.

Quickly flew the allotted month. The last day but
one had arrived, when Edith, whose life was sinking
from anxiety, sent her waiting maid to ask me to see
her. She said, ' You have been faithful to my father,
will you be so to me?' My blood tingled in my veins
as I laid my hand on my heart, and swore that my life
should go for her's.

' Well,' said she, ' provide, then, a companion, and
take me and my maid to Shap Abbey, at twelve o'clock
to-night.' I readily promised what was required, and
kept my word. At early dawn, therefore, we knocked
at the door of the venerable pile. The Abbot, a friend
of the late Sir Arthur's, was astonished at Edith's early
visit. She threw herself at his knees, imploring his
protection.

She and her maid were lodged with the porter, not
being admitted into the holy edifice. The Abbot and
monks in conclave soon determined that whatever their

suspicions might be, they could not withdraw her from
the care of her uncle ; but that she should be safely
accommodated at Bampton Grange with the wife of the
steward of their beautiful possessions, until measures
might be taken as to finally disposing of her.

Nicholas having ascertained the place of his niece's
refuge, after having searched vainly for some time,
came with his son fretting and fuming to the Abbey.
Neither the sacredness of the place, nor the venerable
Abbot, could control the ire of the irascible Wilsons.
At last the brotherhood consented to surrender. Edith
at the expiration of two months to embrace a religious
life ; and in the meantime she was to prepare for so
solemn a dedication of herself to the service of Holy
Church.

Frequently would Edith now watch the path down
the valley, in the hope of seeing young Thornburgh,
but in vain,—until at last she doubted his faith, and
hope gave place to despair. Still she would often recall their hours of sweet intercourse, and his imagined
death would overwhelm her.

Days passed thus, and Edith tried to reconcile herself to her fate ; but a loathing of the future would
overspread her soul, when she gazed in memory on the
handsome features and noble bearing of her beloved
Thornburgh,—and heard the soft tones of his voice, as
he had uttered at parting, ‘ Farewell, darling, faithful-
ness is embossed on my sword belt ; and the same word
is engraven on my soul. The one is for my honour, the
other is for mine Edith.’

The two months expired, without tidings having been
received of Thornburgh—but Nicholas remembered the
hour to a fraction. The morn had risen with unclouded
splendour, as the sunlit shadow coloured the tomb-
stones of lady abbesses with the hues wherewith it was

dyed in passing through the gorgeously stained windows of the chapel of the Nunnery, that stands on the banks of the Eden near to Kirkoswald. The altar was studded with waxen tapers; wreathes of flowers hung on every projection in the sacred edifice, the floor was matted with new rushes, and every countenance present awaited with anxiety the entrance of her who was to be immolated for life in the order of St. Agnes.

Then rose upon the ear the voice of subdued melody, as the solemn procession marched up the aisle to the altar :—

> Hark! a voice from heaven descending,
>   Clothed with majesty and love,
> Bids all nations lowly bending,
>   Yield their hearts to God above.
>
> Thus the red-cross-knight, on hearing
>   Cries for aid from Judah's fanes,
> From his bridal altar tearing,
>   Seeks God's foes on eastern plains:
>
> Thus the blood-sprent victor, feeling
>   Crowns and conquests all are vain,
> Finds the cloister's calm, a healing
>   Sacred balm for soul-felt pain.
>
> Thus the vestal maiden, seeing
>   In the Lamb a thousand charms,
> Home and earthly friendships fleeing,
>   Yields her life to Jesu's arms.
>
> Lowly waiteth now before thee—
>   Lord of Heaven—a virgin bride,
> While on earth, may she adore thee,
>   And in bliss reign at thy side.

Yes, and Edith was there, clothed in beautiful array. The floral offerings of her companions had been twined into garlands round the victim; and her own gems were lustrous in her golden hair. But why was the lovely one herself so pallid? Care, disappointment, and persecution had driven the blood from her wasted and death-like cheeks.

The ceremony proceeded—the flowers were removed from the offering. Next the senior sister took the consecrated scissors to cut off her golden tresses, but her hand trembled and she started back, terrified by the thundering knocking at the chapel-door, sounds which had succeeded to the rapid and heavy rattle of hoofs.

In rushed, in frantic haste, a mail-clad warrior, whose whole appearance evinced the speed of his journey. His hand grasped his sword, as he hurried up the aisle, and in impetuous language he cried, as he faced Wilson,—

"Nicholas Wilson, I charge thee as a traitor and a villain, in presence of these sisters—witnesses for God—"

"Hold, thou impious man," said the Lady Abbess, "it becometh not us to hear such profane words in this sacred building."

"Pardon, holy Mother," replied the warrior, "my tongue saith not what, on ordeal, my sword shall not prove."

A shriek rose from the altar—the voice of the knight, though subdued to the lowest murmur that rage and excitement could brook, had betrayed him, and with a cry of "Oh God, 'tis Ralph," Edith sunk on the ground.

"Forgive this youth," said Nicholas Wilson, advancing to the Abbess, "he knows not what he does; but let not his interference prevent the conclusion of the solemn rites in which we are engaged."

Ralph heard him not—his iron arm was supporting the lovely form of his betrothed—and his raised visor showed the intensity of agony with which he gazed on the lifeless figure. The sisters advanced to bear her to their apartments. The two Wilsons, with wrathful countenances, approached Thornburgh, and upbraided him with his audacity. His spirit shrunk from the encounter of reproach—not words but deeds, were then

his motto. He threw down his gage, and addressing
them said, " Take that up, and I pledge myself before
this solemn assembly to prove ye both villains, cowards,
and traitors, and if ye deny it now, ye lie in your
throats."

Neither father nor son replied. Summoned before
the Lady Abbess, with intense interest, she obtained
the information, that as soon as he had received one of
Edith's letters, the first having never reached him, he
hurried homeward, covered with honours from the
hard foughten fields of Grenada—where he had been
engaged with the infidel Moors. Reaching Kendal,
new tidings had almost maddened him; he knew but
one way to avert the fate of his betrothed, and that was
to prove her plighted vow to himself. He hastened to
the apartment of Father Gervase, which had been dis-
used ever since that good old man's death; and there,
making strict search for what he knew to have been
once deposited in the keeping of the priest, he discovered
in an oaken chest a duplicate of the document he
sought, with the signatures of the parties, and the
priest's attestation affixed. With these, moreover, he
discovered instructions for a will, in Sir Arthur's own
hand writing, from which Father Gervase had evidently drawn the real will, which had undoubtedly been
destroyed by Nicholas. With these documents he had
ridden like the hurricane, dreading that he would be
too late to avert the sacrifice. Hearing these irrefrag-
able proofs, the Abbess permitted him to see Edith,
whom proper means had restored to consciousness.

Too cowardly to assert their valour, and unable to
prove their integrity, the Wilsons sneaked away from
the country, while Ralph and Edith, united in holy
matrimony, became examples of domestic happiness.
They resided alternately at Selside Hall and the Black

Hall, their respective inheritances, being renowned at each for their hospitality and charity.

To follow the history of Nicholas Wilson and his son Mark.—The one was carried off by the plague, and the younger lived as an outcast and vagabond, having exhausted his means by profligacy and sin. But one hope remained to him, which was that Edith might die in child birth, and ere that event, which being shortly expected should take place, he resolved to go disguised to the abode of peace and joy, and see for himself. Arrived at Kendal, he was irritated to learn that his hopes to succeed as heir to the property of the Wilsons, would, probably, in the common course of events, be frustrated, and his wicked soul brooded with disappointed rage.

'Twas late one evening, when Edith received a message that a dying old man wanted consolation and sustenance. Ever open to the cry of the needy, Edith put on 'her robes for visiting the sick applicant ; her maidens in vain dissuaded her, urging that her husband was absent, and her health was delicate. She replied that she was bound to pity others, as she hoped to get pity in Heaven. On arriving at the cottage where the sick man lay (which was near to the Kent Side, at the foot of Kemp's yard), a large ugly black dog opposed her entrance. "Down, Nick, down," said the sick man with a feeble voice. The man had a dark countenance, not much furrowed, with a white beard that seemed to have weathered at least four score winters. After hearing his tale, and giving him some refreshing food which she had brought with her, she was about to return when the decrepid patient started up, seized a dagger, and aimed a blow at his angel-like visitor. Edith, terrified, rushed out, but in vain. The dagger was too true to its aim, and she fell lifeless. The assassin disappeared. I cannot describe the agony of her friends. Next day I and others heard that the dog had been seen in the neighbourhood; we tracked it, and among the bushes in Gilling-grove, we found the aged miscreant. He crouched, like a criminal and dastard as he was, before us, and was seized,—while his dog skulked, growling and whining, like a demon, by his side. Divested of his disguise, he, to our amazement, proved to be Mark Wilson.

The law soon afterwards claimed and had its due, and the wretch was hung near the spot where his vile crime was perpetrated. His gibbet has scarcely been removed a dozen years. The moment his life ceased, the dog, who was still his constant attendant and friend, gave a horrible yelling howl and disappeared.

Since that time the form of Edith has occasionally been seen, with the spirit of Mark in the form of a black dog, compelled to follow her; and as oft as he passes the place by the water side, where his felon frame rotted in irons, he is doomed to suffer again the agony of dying.

The brave Ralph Thornburgh, Edith's disconsolate husband, entered the monastery of Shap, and occupied the remainder of his days in pious meditation and alms-giving."

———

BLACK HALL, STRICKLANDGATE.—This ancient mansion, the residence of the Wilsons for many generations, still remains, though shorn of nearly every vestige of its former importance, having been completely modernized by the introduction of sash windows, &c., about fifty-two years ago. It stands on the east side of Stricklandgate, its only noticeable feature, exteriorly, at present being a massive, circular, limekiln-looking stack of chimneys; and is now a busy brush

manufactory, in the occupation of Mr. Rainforth Hodgson.—
Henry Wilson, Esq., Kendal's First Alderman (A.D, 1575-6),
presented to the Corporation two splendid silver flagons,
or drinking cups, engraved with his name and a suitable
inscription: these, together with some other plate, their
successors sometime during the "dark ages" of art — to
their eternal disgrace be it spoken — exchanged for a set of
trumpery candlesticks!! The flagons, when filled to the
brim with spiced wine, smoking hot (as the custom was in
those dear old times), would, we may be sure, figure pro-
minently in this "his Worship's hall so old" on many a
civic gathering of Harry the First, his "Brethren, and
Assistants."

THE RAID OF PRINCE CHARLES.

AN INCIDENT OF 1745.

The peaceful town of Kendal had been for several
weeks kept in a constant state of alarm. Daily accounts from the north had threatened it with an early
visit from the rebellious Highlanders, led on by Prince
Charles Edward Stuart. The fall of Carlisle, and the
inactivity of General Wade at Newcastle, at length
decided the uncertainty; and at two o'clock on the
afternoon of the 22nd of November, 1745, the first division of the Scottish army entered Kendal.

The population, who crowded out to behold the invaders—for curiosity was as active here then as now—
were astonished to find them far less savage in aspect
than they had apprehended. So fearful indeed had
been the rumours of the barbarous character of the
Caterans, that most of the respectable inhabitants had
sent away the females of their families into the remotest
and most sequestered valleys.

The body that now entered, it is true, consisted main-
ly of the Lowland regiments, whose accoutrements were
tolerably complete, and such as wore the kilt were
gentlemen of the clans Alpine and Glengary, who
made a remarkably warlike appearance. But far different were the arms of the division that followed next
day; hundreds possessing only a club, a scythe, or a
dirk.

The appearance of the first noble-looking Gaels inspired the Kendalians with a feeling of respect for them

and for their chieftains, and many a soft eye that peeped from behind a half-closed shutter, looked a second
time at the manly forms of these intrepid mountaineers,
marching to the shrill tones of their native pibroch.
Quarters were soon found for the division, and their
orderly behaviour gained for them the sympathy of
their hosts. Their manners, however, were little in
unison with English habits, and many curious circumstances occurred. We are told of one bold fellow who,
remarking the sparing measure given by the maid-at-
tendant, out of the mustard-pot, to his fellows, took it
from her hand, and with evident gusto exclaimed,
"Her nainsel mun hae muckle o' what is sae gude."
A *spoonful* followed into his mouth and his nasal organs,
and ludicrous contortions soon manifested the suffering
which his ignorant greediness had self-inflicted. Yet,
although such instances of simplicity awakened the
kind interest of the townspeople, the remains of ancient
border hatred towards the Scots was too strong to permit any co-operation with them on the part of the people of Kendal. A few were found, nevertheless, who
could not blind their eyes to the strong claims of the
Stuarts—regarding the government as an hereditary,
divine-right possession—to the British throne ; and it
was in the house of one of this class that young Ronald
Macdonald found himself quartered.

Descended from an ancient clan, Ronald possessed all
the patriarchal nobility of soul which distinguished the
true Highland gentleman. Nephew to the head of his
house, he was beloved by his followers, and upon the
rising, in favour of the Stuarts, he had got a major's
commission in the army which was organised for the
expulsion of the family of Guelph from Britain. He
had not before visited England, but a two years' campaign in the French service had made him acquainted

with the rules of war, and with the refined habits of polite life. It was with perfect ease and dignity, therefore, that he returned the salutations of his host, who welcomed him to a venerable looking house in the low part of Highgate. The elderly gentleman, for such his host was, bore every appearance of having seen military service; and the amputated arm, with the vacant coat-sleeve suspended by a cord from his collar, testified that he had been present and mingled in the strife wherein broad-swords had dealt blows of death. With this veteran Ronald soon found himself at home; nor were his feelings less pleasurable when his host's daughter, the only child of a beloved but departed wife, descended into the parlour to preside over the ample tea-table, at a meal to which the young major, after his march from Penrith, did full justice.

The evening pibroch summoned Ronald at an early hour to the inspection of his followers; and his absence was a time of serious consultation on the part of his host and daughter, as to whether they could confide their sentiments to the young chieftain. As the Scots were to march early on the morrow, Macdonald soon returned, having seen his orderly followers dismissed to their rest. For himself, the interesting company into which chance had thrown him, prevented his seeking repose, and the lengthening hours of night only made the conversation and intercourse of the trio more mutually delightful.

Supper being ended, the aged host poured out a bumper of claret, passed the bottle to his guest, and then, with a solemn inclination of his head, drank to the health of "The King." Ronald joined, giving to the toast what in his view was its legitimate meaning, and proposed returning the salutation by filling his glass to his fair hostess.

"No, no, my dear Sir," said her father, " she and I
had resolved not to disclose our opinions to you, but
your conversation has overcome my prejudices, and I
cannot longer refrain from claiming my right to give
another pledge, in which Bertha will be more glad to
join than receive your compliment."

He then uttered with earnest devotion, in which his
daughter heartily joined, " Prosperity to the Prince, on
his pathway to Royal Westminster."

Their guest was astonished : but he recovered his
surprise in time to form the third in a festive prayer,
as hearty as ever was breathed by a loyal subject for an
adored sovereign.

We cannot detail the explanations which followed
this avowal of fealty to a common liege lord. Ronald's
spirit was kindled within him, as his host detailed to
him the history of the campaign which he had under-
taken when quite a boy, in the memorable rising of
1715. Perhaps Ronald's emotions were increased by the
presence of one of nature's fairest forms. Bertha's was
the loveliness of young womanhood, and her beauty
was not that of expression only. Every feature was
marked and refined. She was tall, but not masculine;
an aristocratic air and dignity reigned in her every
movement, and the partly foreign and partly English
style of her attire, combined to adorn a figure which
might have vied with the models of early Greece. She
was an object fit to be revered by the affectionate devotion of a kindred soul; and the stranger, while he
admired, could not but be amazed that such talent and
such loveliness should be found in so humble a dwelling. The bugle of the cavalry broke on the ears of
the trio, ere Ronald had been willing to seek his bed,
and at three o'clock the chilly air of a November morning hung like dew upon his heated brow.

The march was commenced, and the clashing of claymores, the sound of the pipes, the military password, and the busy hum of the mustering troops, amid which he had to marshal his own division, were so sudden a transition that Ronald could hardly believe that the hours of his sojourn in Kendal had been anything but a dream. In general he was particular in noticing the country, but as he marched that day, nought attracted his thoughts but the absorbing and yet bewildering remembrance of his last night's quarters.

The inhabitants of Kendal, favourably impressed with the first of their visitors, viewed with no dread the arrival of the second division, and as the Chevalier St. George rode up the street, his royal air and manly mien were welcomed by some huzzas, while the hat of many a gazer was doffed as he passed. No accession, however, was gained to his forces during the Sunday which the Prince spent in the town, although the impression in his favour was strengthened by his behaviour, and by that of his officers, who attended the church to hear the sermon of Mr Crackanthorpe, the master of the grammar school (Dr. Symonds, the Vicar, having fled from fear), where they gave very liberally, both of gold and silver, to the collection for the poor, at that time regularly made by persons standing beside the door with pewter plates.

Greatly to the disappointment of the Paul Prys, whose watchful eyes were on the alert, even at this early era of our history, no one was 'spied in communication with the invaders. One, more persevering than the rest, would have it, however, that the stranger gentleman with one arm was seen entering the large house in Stricklandgate, (now—1868—occupied by E. Busher, Esq.,) where the young Prince abode during his stay.

We will not accompany Ronald in his adventures

throughout the remaining course of that ill-fated expedition, during which Preston, Manchester, and Derby
saw the troops advance and retreat, with a feeling approaching to indifference. We will not do more than
allude to Charles Edward's unwillingness to turn back,
which was as difficult to overcome as that of many of
his dauntless leaders, foremost amongst whom was
Ronald, who little brooked retreating before he had
measured his broadsword with the weapons of the
Hanoverian troops. Still his heart was not unmoved
as he bethought him of once again occupying quarters
under that venerable roof, in bonny Westmorland,
where he had been so hospitably entertained.

After the last division of Charles Edward's troops
had marched southward through Kendal, the usual
quietness of the place was resumed, interrupted only by
an occasional detachment of Highlanders following the
Prince into Lancashire. The rumour of Ronald's host
having been in communication with the Pretender had
not, however, been forgotten; and it was singular how
it became more or less a matter of conversation, according as the intervals were longer or shorter between the
passing of the several detachments of Highlanders
through the town. When, however, the Kendal trades-
men had received intelligence from their correspondents
in London,—and a letter from the banking-house of
Smith and Co., to a manufacturing firm, communicated
the first tidings,—that the Duke of Cumberland with
an army of Hessian and other German troops had land-
ed, and were proceeding to give battle to the Scottish
forces; and when this news had been confirmed by a
letter from a Kendal manufacturer, who, from the state
of the country, had been cooped up at Chester with his
goods, afraid to trust himself abroad, and who gave the
further information that the Scots troops had begun a

homeward march, then it was that rumour and suspicion got head, and the authorities began to agitate the question, whether the stranger gentleman, with one arm, should not be put under arrest. The Mayor thought that such a step would be most desirable, as it would show to the reigning monarch the loyalty of the Corporation. Such zeal against all sedition and privy conspiracy on their part might probably obtain further valuable additions to their charter. He said that his counsel was given purely for the honour and safety of the realm ; and he *did not* say that his "lady mayoress" had whispered behind the curtain that loyalty was sometimes rewarded with knighthood, and that *Sir* John Shaw would sound remarkably well. We strongly opine that the sage advice of this worthy and unambitious couple would have been followed, but for the intervention of the town-clerk, a most important functionary—like all town-clerks, by the way—who might, on this occasion, have claimed the merit of being saviour to his town ; for had so decided a step been taken, in addition to the subsequent attack upon the retreating army, we question whether the Scots would not have thought themselves bound to return the compliment by pillaging the place.

It was the opinion—and his advice accorded with that—of this right arm of the body corporate, that, as yet, the decisive battle had not been fought, and that, perchance, the Prince might still win the day, as he had done at Preston-Pans : in which case, he argued, the worthy municipal dignitaries of Kendal might have to pay heavy fines for imprisoning one of his adherents, and at any rate, under the most favourable circumstances attending the progress of the Duke of Cumberland, the defeated army must return through Kendal ; and however his worshipful the Mayor might be willing

to risk his own life for the reigning royal family, he,
himself, like Falstaff, deemed "discretion the better
part of valour." Therefore, he submitted, it would be
more prudent, as well as more consistent with their
duty to their neighbours, to await the tide of events,
and take that course only which would ensure the
safety of the members of the Corporation, whose lives,
—and he said it very humbly,—were essential to the
prosperity of their native town, and for that reason
worth the lives of all the inhabitants together.

Although such was eventually the decision of the
authorities, some of the inhabitants, more officious than
wise, deemed it needful to send sundry secret letters to
the Government in London (of which the Mayor himself afterwards acknowledged his cognizance), drawing
their attention to a certain suspicious individual resid-
ing in the neighbourhood. Some said that envy at
the admiration which Bertha's charms were obtaining
from the *beaux* of the town, aggravated the loyalty of
the very numerous class of maiden ladies who *then* resided in Kendal, and whose persevering insinuations
fomented in no small degree the antipathy felt towards
the damsel and her father.

Through a friend at Court, the obnoxious individual
soon became aware of these letters, as well as of the
lurking intention to arrest him without form of law,
and it was with utter consternation, that early one
morning, "his worshipful" received tidings of the
sudden disappearance of the stranger and his daughter.
Those who love better to superintend the business of
their neighbours than their own, were now more busy
than ever. Even they who before had hinted that the
one-armed gentleman was hardly dealt by in the suspicions cast upon him, prudently affected to have been
always convinced in their own minds that he would

turn out to be nothing better than a traitor. A thousand circumstances, before unnoticed and perfectly harmless in themselves, were remembered as damning proofs of his guilt, and even the Mayor, whenever he met the town-clerk, looked askance, and thought with grief that "Sir John" was now a visionary and hopeless phantom.

On Saturday, the 14th of December, news was received of the speedy approach of the rebels, in full retreat. It was the market-day when the first division entered the town, and many of the country people were then assembled on their ordinary business, besides numbers whom the proclamation of the Lord Lieutenant had summoned to obstruct the retreat of the Chevalier's army.

As the Duke of Perth's carriage drove in, accompanied by a hundred hussars, just at that part of the town where the Newbiggin narrowed the street into two channels, a shot from a window struck and killed one of his servants. The man fell to the ground, and his horse was immediately seized by some individual who galloped off with it, and escaped both detection and pursuit. Perhaps the thief thought that the spoil of war was no robbery, when he afterwards found a large sum of money in the portmanteau fastened to the saddle of the horse. But the Duke of Perth, irritated by this attack, instructed his cavalry to return the fire, by way of intimidation—taking care however that the discharge should produce no other effect than that of ruffling the placid, motionless wintry air around. Still the defiance was sufficient to arouse the ire of those who were gathered in the streets; and fresh provocation having been given, the hussars could not be restrained from a second discharge of their carbines, when one individual fell dead on the spot,

Q

and some others were more or less wounded. This dispersed the multitude, and the Duke's detachment proceeded onward, and took up their quarters. The bodies of the poor fellow who was slain and of those who subsequently died of their injuries, it may be added, were afterwards interred in the grave-yard of the Parish Church, near the river, where a tombstone was erected at the public expense to commemorate the event.

Before night the main army of the Scots arrived. Their anger was naturally aroused by the tidings of the attack which had been made upon Perth's troop, and they threatened destruction to the town. Their feelings probably had been soured by the compulsion of an unwilling retreat ; and hence the conduct of the people of Kendal was in their eyes more base than it might otherwise have appeared, and so was declared to call for vengeance.

Lord Elcho, being commissioned by the Chevalier to settle the mode of retribution, on him the Corporation now waited to endeavour to avert or mitigate their punishment. He met them in the Moot Hall, and it was galling indeed to the municipal dignitaries to become suppliants in the arena of their own greatness. With the best grace they could assume, however, they told his Lordship that the attack had been made by country people, over whom the officers of the town had no control; and they very humbly prayed, that "his Royal Highness the Prince" would mercifully pass over the offence. It was heart-rending work for Mr John Shaw to give the appellation of royalty to the "Pretender." Alas! thought he, after this I shall never see the gleam of the sword of knighthood waving over my head—Mrs. John Shaw will certainly never be "my lady!" and henceforth I shall be the

victim of conjugal unblessedness. With much entreaty the body corporate—carrying their cocked-hats
in the most orderly manner under their arms—besought
Lord Elcho to commute their punishment into a money
fine. When, however, five hundred pounds was demanded, the whole corporation, town-clerk and all,
lifted up their hands in such amazement, that Elcho
could hardly believe that the town itself possessed five
hundred pence.

Most plaintively did "his Worship" assure "his
Lordship" that they were but a set of poor cloth-weav-
ers, skinners, and tanners; and that so heavy a sum
could hardly be raised in the whole county—so barren
was it and sterile; that they were bounded by moorlands on every side, and that with difficulty could they
obtain a single hundred guineas.

Wearied at last with the tedious details of corporate
poverty submitted to him, Lord Elcho decided that the
town should pay one hundred and fifty guineas. The
mayor and his companions begged hard for two days to
raise the money, hoping, doubtless, that in the meantime the chapter of accidents would produce some turn
in their favour. The request, almost against expectation, was granted; for as the rear-guard was following,
they, it was foreseen, could receive the amount. The
next day, accordingly, the rear-guard, commanded by
Lord George Murray and Colonel Roy Stuart, with the
soldiers of the Glengary clan, and some of the artillery,
entered the town. The penalty was of course then demanded, but it was not without hard pressure that the
worthy burgesses could be prevailed on to contribute
their quota; nor then without making several deduc-
tions touching sundry pairs of shoes, which had been
taken, warm from the feet of the townspeople, by the
Highlanders, who were much in want of that article of

apparel. At last, however, the whole sum of one
hundred and fifty golden guineas was counted down to
the rigorous "rebels," and the troops prepared to
pursue, on the morrow, their cheerless route to the
North.

Ronald's feelings were of no common character as he
quitted Kendal early on the morning of Wednesday,
the 18th of December. The affairs which he had been
required to superintend had demanded much attention,
during his stay in the town, but his engagements had
not prevented him from seeking his former quarters,
where, to his dismay, he learned that Bertha and her
father had left. He ascertained that their principles
had been the cause of their departure, but to conjecture
the place of their retreat was in vain.

Wherefore did the casual acquaintance that had
taken place, now so powerfully influence his feelings?
The reciprocal interest which he and his host felt for
the fortunes of the Stuarts, could not be the only cause;
—many surrounded him with whom he held those feelings in common; yet no sentiment, beyond that actuat-
ing ordinary compatriots was the result. Could it be
that Ronald now experienced the power of Bertha's
beauty and intelligence? Could it be that he was
sensible to a communion of heart during their brief
intercourse, and that already a free-masonry, so to call
it, of feeling had been established between them? Was
it that he not only loved, but dreamed that he was also
beloved?

Weary and long seemed his wanderings that day
over the barren fells of Shap. The troops he commanded were depressed in spirit. Theirs was a retreat without the excitement of an enemy immediately in the
rear, and the solitariness of the march, much of which
was before sunrise, while it seemed to remind them of

their native heath-land, left them also at leisure to re-
flect, with dismay, on the past and on the future.

The group of respectable houses which constituted
the village of Shap, formed a pleasant break upon their
thoughts. Here they stayed awhile for rest and refreshment, and to gather up the stragglers of a preceding division, who had been detained by the breaking
down of some of the ammunition waggons.

Unquiet and thoughtful, Ronald strolled out of the
village to rest himself, apart from his companions. He
had sat down on a stone near a farm house, when he
saw a figure approaching him. He looked up vacantly,
and, in reply to an enquiry for news, briefly said, that
the troops were marching to Carlisle.

He was effectually aroused, however, by the stranger
saying, " Glengary, do you know me ?"

Yes—he knew that voice on the instant—the tones
—familiar as those of a father—belonged to his Kendal
host.

Ronald grasped the old man's hand, and eagerly inquired where he and Bertha had chosen their concealment.

" In this neighbourhood," said the gentleman, adding
that he had only ventured out for the purpose of obtaining, if possible, some direct intelligence respecting the
retreat, concerning which he had heard most confused
accounts.   Ronald asked after Bertha's health; he
wished also to send her a message, but his tongue
faltered,—the pibroch told him that the troops were
about to resume their march ; and, feeling as if they
were about to part for ever, he clasped her father's
hand, with a heartfelt " God bless you," and hastened
away to disguise his feelings, and to resume his wonted
composure before rejoining his followers, among whom
he felt that his looks of abstraction and care had already

diffused feelings of gloomy discouragement. He would gladly have returned to join the fugitives in their hiding place, and have thrown the future to the winds; but his honour, his prince, and his clan required his devotion, and he resolved to banish all remembrance of the vision, which for awhile had entranced him. Moreover, events were thickening around him, which absorbed his whole man; for an officer who had been left with a small company of cavalry at Kendal to await tidings of their pursuers, galloped up soon after their departure from Shap, to announce the speedily expected arrival of the advanced guard of the pursuing army.

The effect produced on the Highland army by the intelligence of the near approach of their pursuers was marvellous. It was like the announcement of game to the hunter. Each man grasped his claymore as if to be sure it was at his side, and the merry jest, the cheerful Jacobite song, and expressions of renewed confidence now rang from man to man. To Ronald the tidings were most opportune. The sudden, and as he supposed, final termination of his acquaintanceship with Bertha, imparted to him a feeling of reckless valour, and he now wished only for a soldier's honourable grave, as if nothing else were worth living for.

Very shortly the chasseurs of Kingston's regiment were seen approaching, and nothing prevented the Scots being attacked but their firm phalanx, and the steady order of their march. On the open moor, or the elevated grounds, or wheresoever the cavalry had a chance of taking them in flank, small detachments were separated, who covered the advance of the main body, until the whole had passed onward. In this service Ronald and his followers were peculiarly conspicuous. They often waited till the cavalry were almost within gunshot, who durst not charge the levelled muskets of the Highlanders, standing, as firm as their own red deer, at bay.

In this way was the march conducted until evening. Lord George Murray had received from the Chevalier directions to join the main army at Penrith, as speedily as possible. He had sent Colonel Roy Stuart to the Prince to ask for a reinforcement to keep the King's troops in check. He saw the necessity of this step, and though unsupported, he immediately resolved to take up his ground, and face his pursuers.

The favourable opportunity of arresting the advance of the foe soon occurred;—the hamlet of Clifton was found to be occupied by some local militia, hastily assembled to oppose the retreat. These fled at first sight of the Scots. Lord George, at once seeing the advantages of this locality, placed his troops, amounting, with the addition of straggling detachments, to about one thousand men, along the hedges from the church down to the Park wall of Lowther Castle. Ronald and a part of the Glengary regiment were stationed where the Park wall almost abuts upon the road. Silence pervaded the scene, except when the blast bore on its wings the sound of distant horsemen. The clouds hurried rapidly athwart the sky, sometimes veiling the moon in darkness, and then as suddenly opening a passage for her beams to shine with the brilliancy of daylight. The clans were now going to enjoy what they had long desired, and the stillness of night daunted not their courage. Their general went from station to station, and in reply to his whispered inquiry of "Ready?" he everywhere met with the determined answer of "Aye, sir, musket and broad-sword."

As a sudden gleam of moonshine was faintly dying away, Murray perceived the figures of dismounted dragoons advancing through the fields and along the

road. He knew that for the Highlanders it was
necessary that they should be the assailants. He waited
but a moment, every breath was held, only the measured tread of the dragoons was heard. They halted, as
if to inspect the position of the foe. At that juncture,
Murray called to the Macphersons and Stuarts to advance. The order was barely uttered, when the blaze
of fire from the advancing columns disclosed their
formidable number. Ere the peal had died away,
Murray shouted " Claymore!"—that war cry which to
the Highlanders means death to the knife—and un-
sheathing his own, he dashed forward at the head of
his troops upon the enemy below.

The shock was tremendous; the dragoons in vain
tried to hold their ground, for the northern broad-
swords crushed their helmets, and gave fearful death-
wounds at a stroke. The Macdonalds saw their leader
heading the attack, with Ronald at his right hand.
The chieftain of Glengary was now attacked by a
horseman, whose position gave him many advantages,
and he would soon have perished, had not Ronald
drawn upon himself the attention of the mounted assailant, who was now aided by two dragoons. The conflict was unequal, and Ronald fell covered with wounds,
but not till the enemy had been driven, in all directions,
off the field, and his assailants themselves had shared
his fate, being cut down by the men of his own clan,
who had seen their major fall. The night had now
become darker than ever. Rain began to fall fast, and
having repulsed this body of pursuers, amounting to
nearly four thousand cavalry, Lord George immediately
drew off his forces towards Penrith, leaving the honoured dead and wounded upon the field.

We must now recur to Ronald's Kendal host, who
after his interview near Shap, speedily returned to a

farm house in Rossgill, where Bertha was awaiting his intelligence.

Distressed as she had been at the retreat of the Scots army, her apprehensions were fearfully increased by the dread that a few hours would bring on a conflict between the parties. Her anxiety was more intolerable from knowing that she could not help her friends, and she burst into tears, with the exclamation, " Father, would to God that your arm had been preserved until this day, or that you could inspire me with your spirit, then the Prince would have had another defender against those murderous Hanoverians." The distant approach of a foraging party from the troops who were now passing through Shap, warned Bertha and her father of their need to leave the house to which they had only come that day for information.

They hastened their departure, therefore, to a more remote retreat, and had passed the foot of Knipe Scar ere they heard the distant sound of musketry fired into the bushes by the troopers, lest any Scots should be lurking amongst them. While Bertha shuddered, the reports seemed to act upon her father as the sound of the trumpet does upon the war-horse. He stopped his steed, turned to his daughter, and said, " I must—I will—help them."

Vainly she persuaded him to stay. At last she said, "You cannot fight, but you may administer relief to the wounded and dying. Pledge me not to go into the field, and to take Roger, and then I will say Go, and God speed you."

To this her father at last consented, and turning his horse's head, he with his servant sought the pass to the high road over the Scar, while Bertha, giving rein to her pony, galloped homeward to their quiet resting place.

R

Onward however sped her father, following, on the high ground, the march of the royal troops, and when evening closed in, he was still pursuing his way. He had nearly arrived at Clifton, when heavy peals of musketry told him that the ranks were engaged. He put spurs to his horse, and we doubt whether his ardour would not have led him into the affray, had not the quick and confused arrival of mingled foot and horse given him notice of the retreat.

The open ground, along the height, afforded him a road towards the scene of action, and rejoicing in the victory which he perceived had been gained by the Scots, he left his horse with his servant, and proceeded to the spot on foot. In the darkness, the groans of the wounded guided him aright. The armies had retreated in contrary directions, and only a few country people were now on the ground, attempting to remove those who were not yet dead. The sufferers who wore the tartan seemed to excite no compassion; to these the benevolent stranger turned. A group of bodies lay in a part where the trampled and furrowed field bespoke the thickest of the conflict. There he found an officer lying under a horse, his clenched fist still grasping the mane, which he had seized on receiving his death wound. And here was a dragoon, supported by the same horse, with rage depicted in his countenance, as he still retained his position, that of fencing off a blow, although a cut upon his left shoulder to his very heart had nearly severed his arm from his body. It was the stroke of one of the Glengary clan. Alas! thought the veteran soldier, *here* are no wounded, for the contest has been too stern to leave any alive. A lurid light, as the moon shone through a dense cloud while he uttered these words, opened to his view so horrible an expression in the face of the dead dragoon, that he

started back. With his change of position, his eye
caught a glance of the tartan of the clan Glengary.
Ronald rushed upon his memory, and looking upon the
face of the object before him, he recognised the body
of the young major. "Ah!" thought he, "this is a
couch meet for a warrior—the foe for his pillow, the
ensign of the enemy for his shroud (for he found that
was wrapped around him, as if having won it, he clung
to it till the last), and the heavens themselves in
mourning for the brave!" But, was it possible that
life was still remaining! did that breast heave a sigh
—that forehead so cold, did it still beat—that eye, was
it open in mere vacant fixedness? The visitor thought
so, but as he anxiously gazed by the dim light on his
wounded friend, he could hardly believe it.

Bertha had hastened homeward along the rugged
path at the foot of the mountains, which overhang the
north-west side of Hawes Water. As the evening
closed in, the road became scarcely discernible, but her
steed knew the way, and he safely wound around those
mighty rocks, which time and winter storms had
hurled from the impending cliffs down to the very
water's edge.

As she passed over a humble bridge at the entrance
into Mardale, the voice of a hound bayed a welcome,
and she soon found herself in the sequestered abode
which sheltered her parent and herself.

Reader, have you ever visited Mardale Green? If
not, our feeble description will convey an inadequate
idea of the solemnity of its wild grandeur. At the base
of almost perpendicular mountains, lie a few acres of
mossy sward, cut off from the neighbouring vale of
Bampton or Hawes Water, by a rugged rock called
Chapel Hill. Standing in this secluded spot, the eye
can detect no means of exit. A small chapel, one of

those humble temples which adorn our remote districts,
erects its ancient tower at the southern corner of that
shut-up scene. At a farm house not far from the
church, was the dwelling in which Bertha and her
parent felt secure.

On reaching her home, her first business was to prepare for her parent's return. The kind family with
whom they lived, had been indebted to her father for
the life of one of its members, and their attachment
knew no bounds. Bertha had at all times free access
to the hall, whose ample chimney, open to the roof,
and peat fire on the hearth, bespoke the home of the
old Westmorland statesman ; but a small room shut off
from this, enabled her to enjoy privacy.

It was in this closed sort of apartment, adorned with
little more than Bertha's books, her harp, and her
paintings of scenes in the neighbourhood, that she
awaited her father's return, having prepared for him a
blazing fire and warm refreshment. She had two or
three times consulted with farmer Mounsey, as to the
length of time needed to go even to Penrith, and when
hour after hour passed beyond the period stated, and
her father and his attendant returned not, filial anxiety
was stretched to the utmost. No one in the house retired to rest. Twelve and then one o'clock were
sounded by the ancient clock. Often did the murmur
of the wind induce Bertha to run to the door, thinking
it was the sound of the absent ones, but the cold gust
of the north rushed in and chilled her very soul. At
one o'clock two of the sons set out to meet their lodger.
They took the pathway over Fordindale, greatly apprehensive that they should find the absentees wounded, if not killed, at the foot of some cliff of the rugged
Blencrhasset.

Bertha grew more timid and nervous, until at last a

well-known footstep delighted her ear ; she rushed out,
and fell into her father's arms. Coming to the light,
she saw he was jaded and weary, and that his garment
was stained with blood.

Bertha's eyes recovered their brilliancy, as she
glanced proudly upon his brow, and said, " I see that
my father's arm has again been raised for the honour
of his Prince."

" No, my love," he replied, " the stain you have discovered is the blood of the brave youth, who ate of our
bread and drank of our cup, and whom I have again
brought for refuge under our roof."

Bertha started back, crying " Can it be Ronald ?"

Her father briefly explained all ; a couch was prepared, and soon the wounded and insensible Glengary,
accompanied by Roger and the two Mounseys, was
brought to the door, borne on a sort of litter made of
cloaks, suspended between the two horses. The rugged
path, which it was necessary to take for fear of discovery, and the care of the wounded, had made the
journey from Clifton very difficult.

We need not dwell on the care which the young
chieftain received under that roof, nor on the secrecy
maintained by every one in the family, nor on the im-
provement which the patient made, who was now longing to thank Bertha for the many comforts provided
by a thoughtful but unseen hand.

It was one evening in January when Ronald, for the
first time, left his bed-chamber, and joined Bertha and
her father in their little sitting-room. He had changed
his garments to those of a Westmorland dalesman, for
the purpose of security, and this metamorphosis, and
much more his pallid countenance and debilitated appearance, would have prevented a recognition by his
nearest connections. Despite the cold tempest beating

outside their dwelling, the waters of a hundred cata-
racts foaming down the mountain sides, and the snow,
their best guardian, lying in deep and impassable drifts
on every hand, Ronald's countenance, as the cheerful
conversation proceeded in that snug little apartment,
began to assume its usual animation, and his eye its
wonted brilliancy, while he described, with all the
warmth of unchecked love for the Prince and his cause,
the bravery of the clans at Clifton. Bertha listened
with emotions of pity and loyalty, and would gladly
have continued the conversation, but her father, fearing
excitement for the youth in his then delicate state,
suggested an early withdrawal to rest, proposing that
they should first hear one of Bertha's songs.

She took her harp without any affectation of diffi-
dence, and began—

Bright bloom'd the heath on the brow of the mountain,
   And sweet was the incense it raised to the sky ;
Sparkling and strong was the rush of the fountain,
   But lo ! the heath withers—the fountain is dry.

Where is the banner that waved o'er the moorland ?
   And where are the broad-swords that circled it round ?
Where are the thousands that rushed down the foreland,
   Heart-loyal and true, to the pibroch's brave sound ?

Alas ! for the gloaming has shadowed their glory—
   Has dimmed the bright prospects that greeted our eye,
And the sunlight which shrunk from a field dark and gory,
   Leaves a night drear and starless to curtain our sky.

But weep not, loved Albyn, for morning is dawning,
   Thy sons ever faithful, and loyal and brave,
Choose the dark gulf of death in its dread horror yawning,
   Their pathway to glory,—than live as the slave.

What ! though for a moment the foeman has speeded,
   His days are all numbered—his wraith has shone red ;
What, though for a while the true Prince is unheeded,
   The radiance of hope is still over him shed !

What, though if the bird to its own rocky eyrie,
   Hath winged all undaunted its heavenward flight ;
What, though the proud ocean wave, restless, unweary,
   Retreats from the strand where it broke in its might.

The eagle returns again fresh from his fastness,
  And sweeps from the clouds, unrepelled, on his prey;
The ocean re-rolls on the beach in its vastness,
  Nor mortal nor rock its stern coming can stay.
So the night of our sorrow shall dawn into morning,
  The heather re-bloom o'er the moorland and lea,
And the crown of a kingdom its true heir adorning,
  Shall gladden the gallant, the loyal and free.

* * * * * *

Spring time had now awakened the snow-drops from their wintry bed—the snow was gradually disappearing, and with the advance of the season, Ronald's strength was by degrees becoming restored. Many a consultation had been held by the fugitives respecting the way for him to rejoin his clan. Since the fight at Clifton, they had only procured one newspaper, in which he was numbered with the dead. Fear of discovery, and latterly the snow, had prevented any intercourse with the world; and Ronald was entirely ignorant of the proceedings in the North.

A brilliant morning, towards the end of March, at last arrived; the grass was shooting up, and the green leaves of the earliest trees were peeping forth, when Ronald and Bertha, having strolled out, found themselves upon the summit of Chapel Hill.

The day became still, and, for the season, sultry. A bright blue sky was above them, while a dense mass of cloud gradually overspread Naddle forest, throwing an awfully black shadow over that side of the lake, which elsewhere was a perfect calm of emerald hue.

They gazed with admiration upon the scene; Ronald with intense interest, for a messenger had been sent to Penrith to obtain as much information as possible, in order that final arrangements might be made for his departure. Perhaps it might be the last time that he should be alone with Bertha, and he could not resist confessing to her the pain which the thought gave him.

She told him that now the field of honour was his—
that if prosperity awaited their cause, possibly they
might again meet, and added, with the coolness of determined resolve, " Let the rightful heir be again driven
from his inheritance, and this bosom shall not be defiled
by breathing the atmosphere of so faithless a land."

Ronald earnestly urged a similar determination on
his part. His heart beat hurriedly, and he felt the
fatigue of the walk, and the excitement of the interview, acting upon his brain. Bertha marked his flushed
cheeks and his pallid brow now dewed with perspira-
tion, and she thought how little fit he was to encounter
the hardships of a campaign. Her feelings overcame
her, and with tears of affectionate interest, her noble
heart confessed its womanhood, as she replied, scarcely
knowing what she said—" God grant that we may meet
again."

Ronald grasped her hand, pressed it to his lips and
to his heart, while he vowed to be hers for ever.

The sudden flash of distant lightning aroused them
to observe the turmoil of the elements. The cloud on
the east side of the lake had spread southwards until
the whole of Knipe Scar seemed but one curtain of
blackness, while around their own sheltering mountains darkness was fast gathering. Another flash was
like a hand writing characters of light on the escarp-
ment of the Scar, and the thunder pealed from the
mountains of Crossfell. It was high time to hasten
home, although the sky overhead was yet a deep azure,
but ere they had descended half way down the Chapel
Hill, clouds overspread all the heavens. The air felt
like the breath of a furnace. Suddenly a flash gleamed
immediately above them, and straight their own mountains sent forth the note of thunder,—it was reverberated by a thousand echoes,—and then the hollow

sound rumbled up the narrow glens and ravines until it was lost in a distant grumbling over Hill-bell and Harter-fell.

Ronald knew the Highlands well, yet never had he seen aught like this. The black clouds seemed to rest on the peaks of the mountains; beneath them, in the inequalities of the ridges, light peeped through in singular patches. The basin-like valley was itself a picture of gloom, only here and there a lingering snow-drift retaining its whiteness. The rugged brows of the hills looked more fearful than ever, and the waterfalls murmured with a hoarser sound.

Another flash blazed like the burst of a volcano,—it seemed to rive the clouds in twain, and as the ball of fire struck a projecting cliff, the mass gave way, and tumbled down the mountain side: but the crash of its fall was lost in the tremendous peal which followed. The ancient hills seemed shaken to their foundations. Down each gully rushed a current of wind like a hurricane. Rain-drops and hailstones came pouring down, and before Ronald and Bertha could reach home their garments were as wet as if they had been soaked in the lake. The account of the victory of the Prince at Falkirk greeted their return, and stimulated Ronald to a hasty departure; but that night found him in a high fever produced by being heated and then suddenly chilled. Delirium succeeded, under which Bertha was the subject of his incoherent expressions, and it was her care alone, he said, which restored him to health and to the disastrous intelligence of the battle of Culloden, consummating the utter hopelessness of the cause of the Stuarts.

We will not follow up the butchery which ensued after that hard fought engagement; nor enumerate the victims whose blood was poured out to atone for their errors. The doom of the traitor awaited not only those who had followed the Chevalier's standard in that expedition, but the heroes of 1715 were also condemned when captured. Spies, informers, and bribes, ensnared many a fugitive in his secret abode of imagined security.

It was late one evening in August 1746, that three persons clothed in the garb of Westmorland peasants, entered the Bull Inn, in Aldgate, London. A few days sufficed them to make their preparations for departure to the Continent; a friend in office procured them passports, and the Friday evening arrived upon which a vessel was to sail to Boulogne. The parties had already shipped their luggage, and were walking quietly to the wharf in order to go on board before the bustle of weighing anchor. They had reached the London-docks when Ronald, one of the three, unfortunately stumbled against an individual who seemed wrapt in his own thoughts. Ronald's Scotch accent, in asking pardon, attracted the persons attention, who then recognized that the attire of all the three was the costume of his own county.

The incongruity of the language with the garb led him to notice them more particularly, and then, lifting up his hands, he exclaimed, as he looked upon Bertha and her father,—" Good God, it is them!"

His countenance was remembered at once by the two as that of the quondam Mayor of Kendal, from whose persecution they had already suffered. They therefore hastened forward to the good ship " Marié," and went on board, but not before Mr John Shaw, who had followed them, had noticed their destination.

It was singular enough that this worthy personage should now be in London at the recommendation, to use the mildest word, which infers a peremptory com-

mand—of Mrs Shaw, who had been grievously vexed
at not obtaining her hoped for title. She had, by the
force of constant pecking, at last induced "her dear
John" to go to town to seek some remuneration
for his loyal services. His applications had, alas!
been all treated with disdain, and he was meditating
some other resource, to avert the wrath of his wife,
when he met Bertha and her father, which was, in his
opinion, an undoubted God-send.

At eight o'clock the ship "Marié" left the quay
with her passengers, who now deemed themselves safe,
and the vessel was swiftly going down the broad
Thames with the tide, when she was hailed by a boat
which followed them rapidly, having on board some
officers of justice, amongst whom was Shaw, standing
up, and bawling out lustily, "stop the ship." The
helmsman of the boat requested him to sit down, but
elevating the warrant of arrest as if it were the patent
of his promotion, he answered "Hold your peace, I
shall be a baronet soon."

Alas, for him! his august personality had so ob-
structed the sight of the steersman, that a large fishing
smack bore down upon them unperceived, and before
the boat could avoid her, and just as the captain of
the "Marié" was about to shorten sail, the unfortun-
ate Shaw, with boat and crew, were run down by the
smack.

The warrant was washed down the river, but the
would-be baronet and crew were extricated. The
former was half dead with terror, and was most glad to
hurry to a warm bed in his own quarters at the Pig
and Whistle, in Cannon-row, Westminster.

The captain of the "Marié" upon observing the
accident, waited for no further orders, but made the
best of his way, having, as it was suspected, little in-

clination to suffer the revenue officers to test too
minutely the quality of his cargo.

Here our history must have concluded, had not a
pedestrian tourist from Kendal, in the year 1821, been
surprised to see standing at the Brown Cow in Mardale,
a gentleman's carriage. So unusual a sight, as the
road from Bampton to the head of the lake would
hardly admit of more than a cart, roused his curiosity.

He found that it belonged to a venerable French
officer, wearing the Cross of the Legion of Honour,
who was accompanied by a fine looking female of
middle age. On inquiring of their servant more particulars, he learned that the gentleman was visiting the
place where his parents had once resided, and where
his father was wounded.

Further investigation, with a drop of the native,
loosened the servant's tongue, who proved to be a High-
lander, and informed our tourist that the parents of the
officer above alluded to, were Glengary and Bertha,
and that this stranger was the only surviving offspring
of their marriage. It appeared that on taking refuge in
France, Ronald had entered the French service, and that
his son, following his father's fate, after a series of cam-
paigns under Napoleon, had been raised to the highest
military rank, and even obtained the title of Duke and
the Baton of a Marshal of the Empire. Thus, he was
enabled to visit, in company with his daughter, that
Mardale and those Clifton heights, of which, when a
youth, he had heard such romantic histories.

Our tourist believes the servant also told him
that Bertha's father was a younger brother of Lord
Derwentwater's; but of this he is not confident, only
he remembers distinctly that the officer said that
Bertha's name was Ratcliffe, which makes such a pre-
sumption very probable.

DUNMAIL RAISE.

CHAPTER I.

" That pile of stones,
Heaped over brave King Dunmail's bones ;
He who had once supreme command,
Last King of rocky Cumberland ;
His bones and those of all his power,
Slain here in a disastrous hour !"

WORDSWORTH.

Although the summer had not fully waned, the
weather had set in cold and tempestuous as at the close
of autumn. The mountain rills were swollen by frequent showers ; the tarns had overflowed their ordinary bounds ; and the mountain slopes were penetrated
with moisture, yielding like a sponge to the pressure
of the wild deer, or of the venturous hunter who sought
to pursue them into the pathless thickets studding
alike the hills and the dales of rugged Westmorland.

Night had descended over Potter Fell ; and as the
starless darkness closed around, the croak of the wood-
owl, the flapping of the bat, and the occasional hoarse,
deep bark of the wolf, prowling in search of prey, were
echoed discordantly from the crags and peaks that
bounded the horizon. It was a wild and lonely scene.
Man had scarcely yet asserted his reign over the bleak
region—having contented himself with forming here
and there a road through the most favoured tracts, in
order to connect the more profitable domains of Cum-

bria and Scotland with the fertile South:—yet man
was not wholly wanting there, even in that hour of
gloom and desolation. The wild bulls, grazing in the
meads that rise from the margin of the Kent at Burneside, were startled at their pasture, and turned away
from the dusky figures and low muttering voices of two
human prowlers, wending their way towards the hills,
as if anxious to avoid the haunts and to escape the ob-
servation of other men.

As these night-wanderers proceeded—heedless of
the pelting of the mingled hail and rain, and the
muttered thunder which growled around the neighbouring mountain tops—they seemed absorbed in conversation.

"I tell thee, Leolf," said the taller personage, who,
from his tone, seemed accustomed to command, "that
I will seek no shelter more till I be avenged on the
Atheling, who, by treacherous wiles, has obtained a
victory over my brave people, and has disposed
of my realm as if it were a thing of spoil or of ransom."

"It is thine, my lord," said the person addressed,
"to will, and thy servant's to obey. But yet, if I
might urge it, there still be true hearts to whom your
safety might be entrusted. Men who would form a
rampart around you with their bosoms, and who would
spend the last life-drop to restore to you the sceptre
which has been wrested from your hand—would you
but permit them to be informed of your retreat, and to
display your confidence in their fidelity."

"Nay, Leolf—thou judgest of others by thyself. The
accursed Saxon has overthrown our altars, and with
his potent ale has debauched the minds and faith of
our friends and followers, till safety no longer remains
in the land of our fathers."

"Then," argued Leolf, "let us flee at once. Among the bold and hospitable Gael of the far North, you will find a secure home until better days shall enable you to descend to your native valleys, and to sweep your foes from the hill side, as the eagle expels the fox-brood which has dared to encroach upon the precincts of its eyrie."

"I have said," replied the chief speaker:—"In thee alone have I hope for deliverance. To thy hand and thy skill I would trust much, and will trust; such, indeed, is my burning for vengeance, that to rid my country from the presence of these proud and cruel Saxons, I could endure a thousand-fold the misery and degradation which have been heaped upon me. Thou, then, shalt be my messenger—take my signet as thy voucher. I will pursue my wanderings alone, whilst thou, returning to the peopled dales, shalt gather the sentiments, and re-inspire with thoughts and hopes of freedom, such still loyal Britons as aspire to be free from the base bondage of the conqueror."

"But ere I fulfil this mission, my lord, may I not see thee bestowed in the shieling of some trusty Cumbrian."

"Have I not said, Leolf, that no roof shall shelter me more till I have vengeance?"

"Be it so, then, Sire. I will depart with the first rays of the morning's sun."

"Depart at once. Thou knowest every turn of these wild hills and valleys, and, making thy way through the darkness, thou wilt appear, by the morrow, as if from heaven, among those who wilt at least be glad to learn that the price set upon our heads by King Edmund has as yet been in vain to purchase our blood."

It is almost needless to say that the speakers in

this dialogue were Dunmail, King of Cumbria, and his
faithful attendant Leolf, who had been brought up beside him from boyhood ; and who, through every stage
of fortune had followed him and been his stay, when
nobler friends had sought individual safety in flight or
submission. The King, after having taken part in the
great battle of Brunnaburgh against Athelstane, had
made his peace with the conqueror, and after his death
had lived for a while in friendship and good under-
standing with his successor, Edmund the Atheling ;
but the latter, an ambitious and treacherous prince,
remembering the stern opposition encountered by his
father, had gathered an army, about the year 942,
among the Wolds of Yorkshire, giving out that he
meditated an attack upon Malcolm, King of Scotland,
and when he had succeeded thus in lulling to sleep
all suspicion in the mind of the Cumbrian monarch, he poured his desolating host upon the dales of
Westmorland and Cumberland, and reduced Dunmail
to the condition of an exile and outlaw in the very
heart of his own domains. A price had been set upon
the Prince's head—his capital had been laid waste—
the Druid priests of his realm had been remorselessly
massacred, and his people had been enthralled as bondmen to the victorious Saxons. Dunmail had since
wandered among the moors and mountains of his native regions—still hoping, against hope, that an opportunity would arise to call his hardy followers once
more to arms, and enable them to assert the independence of their children and their soil ; and though at
first he had been attended by nobles and courtiers,
bound to him by the sacred ties of kindred and of
gratitude, ere many weeks had passed, he found himself alone with his cupbearer—a fugitive and a vagabond
in the earth.   He found no difficulties in sustaining life.

The red deer, birds of all kinds, and fish were abundant ; and the clefts of the rocks and caverns of the glens afforded ample shelter to one who knew nothing of, or despised the luxuries of delicate fare, of goodly houses, and of the splendid attire which had been introduced into the country originally by the Romans, and which had been adopted, and even rendered more sumptuous, by the sensual Saxons.

The King, it will be readily supposed, however, was not content. His queen and children had escaped into the kingdom of Strathclyde—but they were at a distance from him ; and he, who had been accustomed to obedience from a realm, was compelled to shun the face of the meanest hind, lest he should be betrayed and given up to an ignominious death, from the hands of the hostile stranger. Leolf, therefore, had acquired a sort of ascendancy over his mind ; and his constant urgency to undertake some bold and desperate step was at last successful. The cup-bearer having arranged a future and early meeting, departed ; and Dunmail, amid the darkness of that gusty September night, stood desolate among the hills.

He turned, as his last follower quitted him, and straining his eyes for a moment to watch his course through the thick gloom, bethought him of the number who had gone from his side, since the ebb of his fortune, to return no more. A pang shot through his brain, and a sigh followed ; but, those over, he resumed his onward way up the fell—the storm gradually subsiding as he proceeded, till the muttering thunder sunk upon his ear, and a death-like stillness succeeded. Then the stars, one by one, came forth, twinkling the more brightly for that they had been veiled for a time, and gemming the deep blue of æther, as golden cressets gem an imperial robe.

T

On the top of the fell, amid a grove of dwarf oak,
surrounded with a thicket of birch and ash and hasel,
and studded here and there with a dark-yew, or an
ancient holly-bush, there stood a Druid temple, unde-
faced by the spoiler—a small, rural sanctuary, bearing,
as has been said by a modern author, such relation to
Stonehenge, and the larger monuments of ancient
British worship in England, "that a rural chapel bears
to a stately church, or to one of our noble cathedrals."
At the present day, nothing but the unhewn stones
which formed the inner circle of the temple, with the
sanctuary of justice, remain ; but even these cannot fail
to impress the beholder with some reverence for the
devotion which led his ancestors, established in the
wilderness, to remember the duties they owed to the
Creator and Governor of all things, and to pay Him,
even in the desert, as it were, such homage as consisted
with their knowledge—unenlightened by revelation.

Thither Dunmail bent his steps—without design or
motive, save that the presence of a familiar and vener-
ated object always has a magnetic attraction for such
as feel desolate of heart. He paused amid the mystic
circle, and breathing a prayer to the Lord of Immortality, whose attributes the earliest priests of Britain had
taught in greater purity than either their pagan or
semi-christian successors, sat down within the sanctum
to meditate upon the events which had crowded into
the few past months of his existence, and upon the
prospects of the future.

He knew not how time passed while thus revolving
the bitterness of his fate; but ere he had apparently
rested long, his attention was suddenly awakened by a
dazzling gleam of light, which, diffusing itself throughout the temple, softened gradually into a bright halo,
in the midst of which he perceived a beautiful female

in the snow-white garb of a Druidess, advancing towards him with an attitude of benediction. The heart of the King was filled with awe. He felt that the vision was superhuman, and he knew not what it boded.

"Why art thou here, Dunmail?" asked the apparition. "Why here alone and waking, when other men are housed and asleep?

"Need I answer?" replied the King. "Thou who hast recognised me at first sight cannot require to be told that I have been driven from my throne, to become a joint tenant of the wildernss with the eagle and the wolf."

"Alas, that it should be so," said the sweet and gentle voice of the Druidess. "But thou hast well withstood thine hour of trial in adversity, and brighter days shall dawn upon thy realm and people."

The monarch bowed in silence; for he perceived that the vision was prophetic.

"But thou hast much to achieve," continued the female; "and must have aid in the enterprise. Tell me, then, what would'st thou exchange for thine own deliverance, and for the restoration of thy country's freedom?"

"Even such," said the prince, "as prosperity should yield to me, without injury to others—provided it compromised nothing of my regal duties, or my people's right."

"And should I truly promise to restore to thee thy sceptre, and to bring destruction upon thine enemies, would'st thou follow the counsels I might hereafter whisper into thine ear, when thou shouldest be reseated amid thy flatterers in thy palace festal hall?

"My faith— my life shall be thy pledge."

"It is accepted, prince."

So saying the Druidess drew from her hand a ring,

and placed it on the finger of the fugitive, at the same
time, taking from his neck a small golden ornament,
which in youth had been bestowed upon him by the
Queen, his mother.

"When thou shalt again behold this sign," said the
female, exhibiting before him the golden amulet, "and
shalt be reminded of this night, be sure that the fulfil-
ment of thy promises will be required."

"But stay," exclaimed Dunmail, seeing that the
figure with which he had been talking was about to
retire from the circle—"Stay, I conjure thee, and tell
me——"

The form was enveloped in bright light, and had disappeared from his gaze ere he could finish his entreaty.
He started to his feet, but stumbled in attempting to
rush forward, and when he had recovered himself,
nothing was visible but the hoar trees and the moss-
grown stones, that formed the Druid's circle, around
him, and the paling stars of morning overhead.

CHAPTER II.

The exertions of Leolf to arouse his still patriotic,
though defeated, countrymen, were not made in vain.
The news that the King was still alive and in the
midst of them, and the consciousness of outrage and
wrong, daily inflicted by the victorious Saxons, whose
sole object in retaining the land, seemed to be to ruin
and desolate it, kindled the enthusiasm and loyal
attachment of the dalesmen and mountaineers to a
pitch of frenzy, which indeed could scarcely be restrained until measures might be concerted for such a
general rising against the oppressor as might secure

success to the enterprise. Everywhere new life and energy were displayed, as the returning hope dawned that Cumbria was about to re-assert her ancient independence, and that the hated Saxons would be speedily expelled.

Dunmail was not long left in ignorance of the favourable disposition of his people; but, deprived of the counsel of his faithful and considerate Leolf, he had less prudence, less patient endurance, and less necessary reserve than before; and thus, more than once, he narrowly escaped betrayal into the hands of his foes. He had at all times been accustomed to implicit obedience, and though the circumstances by which he was surrounded required that he should now lay aside his habit of command, he was unable to descend with becoming grace from the sphere of regality to that of common life, which it was absolutely necessary for him to assume, until the moment when the realization of his high projects should no longer be a question of doubtful speculation.

As he traversed the mountain region which surrounds the magnificent lake of Windermere, he was suddenly startled one evening by the appearance of an armed Saxon soldier immediately in his path. He clutched the dirk which hung concealed within his vest, and demanded the purpose of the intruder.

"Thou art a Briton and a stranger," replied the soldier, in the mixed dialect which then prevailed in those districts of England and Scotland, where the near neighbourhood of men whose native languages were entirely different, rendered a common tongue necessary for the purposes of daily intercourse. "A stranger it seems, or despiser of the law which declares the life of a Cumbrian forfeit, should he raise arms against a Saxon freeman."

"You speak boldly," said the king—his lip curling with mingled rage and disdain—"but I would not stain my weapon with base blood. Stand back, and let me pass."

The Saxon was immovable, save that he placed his hand upon the hilt of his sword, or seax, the weapon from which the Saxon name had been originally derived. He surveyed his adversary for an instant from head to foot, then suddenly springing forward to close upon him unawares, he exclaimed:—"I know thee now tyrant. There is a price upon thy head. Thou art my captive."

Dunmail answered not, but sustaining the shock of his opponent's onset firmly, and parrying the blow aimed at him, he clenched his hand upon the soldier's neck, and sought to deprive him of power by mere muscular exertion. In the struggle, however, he dropped his dagger, and seeking to recover it gave his assailant such advantage, that in an instant he lay prostrate upon the moss-grown earth.

"Yield, or thou diest," cried the soldier.

The king, his voice choked with shame and indignation, was unable, even had he been desirous, to reply.

"Thou art he," continued the exulting Saxon, "whose name for the last few days has been bruited through glen and valley, and echoed over mountain and moor, as the saviour, that was to be, of conquered Cumbria. Look thy last, King Dunmail, as thy friends still call thee, upon the bright sun above thee, and bethink of a brief prayer to thy God, for thine hopes and aspirations end here."

The foot of the hostile warrior was upon the breast of the monarch, and his sword was at his throat, when, rushing from behind a crag that jutted into the narrow pass in which the encounter had taken place, a damsel,

young, beautiful, light of foot, and inspired by feelings
compounded of terror and devotion, appeared upon the
scene, and casting herself upon her knees beside the
king, implored the victor for mercy to his captive.

"Nay," said the ruthless savage, "I have fallen upon
a double prize. I was in search of thee, fair runaway,
when I lighted upon this wingless eagle. I will e'en
despatch him first, and then turn to dry thy tears."

"Dastard!" cried the maiden, with vehemence, at
the same time starting to her feet; "Is it not enough
that our homesteads are plundered, and our fields laid
waste by the spoiler; but must rapine and violence
crush at once the prince and the peasant?"

The poniard, which had been dropped by Dunmail,
struck her sight. Quick as thought she seized it, and
ere the Saxon could prepare to ward the blow, plunged
it to the haft in his back. The soldier fell with a
groan to the earth, writhing beneath the mortal agony
with which he had been stricken. There was no time
to lose. The British maiden and the monarch, taking
a route known only to those who had been accustomed
from childhood to tread the intricate windings of the
Westmorland hills and dales, hastened to a place of
safety in Patterdale; where they soon learned that
the wounded Saxon had lived long enough to indicate
to some of his countrymen the direction taken by Dunmail and his fair rescuer, to arouse pursuit, and to
elicit the most solemn vows of vengeance. Rumour,
with her thousand tongues, was busy in every direction. The whole country was disturbed. Here the
Saxons were gathering, at the sound of the bugle, to
hunt the still enfranchised lion in his lair; and amid
the remote dales, there were musterings of the
Cumbrian warriors, eager for freedom, and thirsting
for renown.

Three days passed thus, when on a secret intimation
from Leolf, who amid every difficulty and danger, had
contrived to do his mission warily, and to avert any
direct suspicion, on the part of the enemy, from himself, the beacon was lighted upon Scafell, and, extending thence to Penrith, to Carlisle, to Orton, to Whinfell, and to Helme Cragg, the whole population took
arms, and, marching forth in array, soon joined their
forces, and offered battle to their recent masters.
Songs of liberty, and shouts of patriotic ardour rang
then from every rock and hill.   The *heriban*—or gathering call—sped as if borne on the fleet-winged winds,
over mountain, lake, morass, and scaur; and none
neglected the appeal who was able to wield a spear, a
bow, a sword, or a dirk.   Insult and oppression—
plunder and violation, had filled every heart with re-
vengeful valour, and nerved every arm with gigantic
might.   It was the cause of his home, of his parents,
and his children—of all that was nearest and dearest
to every man—aye, and to every woman, of the
land.

The rising was decisive.   The Saxons, unprepared
for such determined opposition, hastened to retire into
the more settled and amicable counties of York and
Lancaster, without hazarding a blow; and Dunmail,
ere fourteen days had elapsed from the time of his deliverance from death by the golden-haired maiden of
Patterdale—long afterwards celebrated by the native
poets of the north, the *Lakists* of the olden time, as the
fair Guonoline—was reseated in regal pomp upon the
throne of his fathers, in his palace at Appleby—not
then, as now, a place of minor importance, but one of
the first of northern towns in extent, in population, and
in wealth.

The King, elated with success, however, was more

imprudent now that prosperity had returned to him,
than he had been in adversity. Leolf, his faithful attendant, it is true, was by his side, and ceased not to
counsel him right, even to the risk of offending by
his freedom, when he saw that things were done amiss;
but Leolf was no longer the sole companion and con-
fidant of his master; and other influence had obtained
the ascendancy over the mind of Dunmail, which led
him not unfrequently from the path of rectitude and
of duty. He remembered the service of the beautiful
Guonoline, not merely with such gratitude as he ought
undoubtedly to have entertained towards a deliverer;
but a more questionable feeling arose within his breast,
when, in the presence of his assembled chiefs, he seated
her amid them, and placed upon her brow the golden
circlet of nobility. He loved her—if the name of love
ought to be profaned by being applied to a passion
which, as well according to the notions of that period,
as those of the present day, was held to be impure; and
he sought occasion from day to day, to repudiate the
wife of his youth—the mother of his children—in order
to make room upon his throne for a younger and more
beautiful bride.

Hence coldness, disputes, and finally, a deadly feud
arose between the King of Cumbria, and the Sovereign
of Strathclyde, the brother of his Queen. In the war
which followed, no advantage accrued to either party,
but resources which ought to have been husbanded,
were wasted, the interests of the kingdom were neglected
or sacrificed, and the Cumbrians, seeing that they were
involved in ceaseless broils, grew discontented and dis-
affected. Still the Queen maintained her cheerless place
upon the throne, and Guonoline, unconscious perhaps
of the mischief her charms had wrought, lived peacefully among her native hills, and sang the songs

U

which she had been accustomed to sing from happy childhood.

Since he had been smitten with his fatal passion for the youthful Guonoline, everything had sped worse than formerly with Dunmail and his people. The public interests were neglected; justice, so far as its administration depended upon the King, was delayed; and, through the evil example of the Sovereign, the forms, and, as an almost necessary consequence, the essentials of religion were abandoned, or remembered only to be derided and scorned—an offence which, however we may scoff at the Druidical worship in these days, was, at the period of which we are speaking, calculated to produce as great an extent of public mischief as infidelity and vice among those who are still looked up to by the bulk of the population, under the Christian Dispensation. It was in vain that the faithful Leolf, from time to time, warned his master of the growing prevalence of evil throughout the land, where wrong stalked abroad unpunished, and outrage passed unavenged. The mind of Dunmail was absorbed by one sole object. For that, could such steps have secured the gratification of his wishes, he would willingly have relinquished his throne, and foresworn his race and country. The bright eye of Guonoline acted upon him as a spell, which he could neither break nor flee from. It held him, like a desperate man brooding on revenge, from effort or care, while the thought of compassing the burning desire within him by turns allured and consumed his soul.

At length, when the well-nursed tortures of his guilty mind had goaded him to exertion, he resolved on a project which promised to compensate for the agonies he had undergone. He summoned his court and council to an assembly at " merry Carlisle," to deliberate upon the state and disorders of the kingdom, and to devise means of successfully opposing all future attempts of the Saxons, concerning a threatened invasion from whom reports were already rife among the Cumbrian dalesmen. The moment seemed propitious. The King had devised a scheme for carrying off the object of his love while her father and friends should be at a distance from home in the service of the State ; and, as if the stars themselves had conspired to favour him, Guonolino herself, unasked and unexpected, attended the great national meeting, at which it was generally believed her country's fate was to be decided. She had thus, as it were, thrown herself into the path of destruction, and courted the doom which had been prepared for her.

The heart of Dunmail leaped within him, his hand trembled, his cheek was blanched, his lips were parched, and his brain grew dizzy, as he placed her beside him on the hill of justice, where the chiefs and people met to assist at a solemn celebration of religious rites before entering upon the secular duties of the assembly. The thought crossed him ever and anon, as the lightning flashes through a mountain-pass, that, ere a few short hours had elapsed, the maiden, who was the delight and envy of all eyes, would be his—his without compromising his regal dignity, or subjecting him to the censures of those who constituted his world—and without the knowledge, the meddling, or the scandal of parents, nobles, or priests.

The ceremonies of that day were a blank to the King. The feast with which it closed was scarcely tasted. The songs of the bards, inciting to spirit-stirring deeds of arms, and holding forth the promise of a blessed immortality to all who should worthily acquit themselves in behalf of their altars and their homes, fell upon his listless ears, for the first time, as sounds that but prolonged the tedious hours till Guonoline should be made to listen to, if not to approve the passion her beauty and heroism had inspired in the breast of her Sovereign.

Never did the sun linger so long in his descent, or the shades of twilight gather so slowly as on that summer's eve. All was in readiness to bear away the unconscious damsel—guards, horses, changes of raiment, and a bower of security upon the shelving banks of the Eden—yet still the daylight loitered on the hills, and the festivities were continued. Guonoline herself was happy. Guileless as a fawn amid the impenetrable glades of the forest, she meditated no evil, and therefore suspected none; but sat amid the courtly group, who honoured her for the sake of their monarch's favour, with the same artless simplicity as when, excited by feelings of loyalty and justice, she had sprung from her lurking place to the rescue of the King from the hands of the ruffian who had been her own pursuer; and when she retired from the scene in company with those for whom her exploit on that occasion had procured the rank of nobility, it was with feelings of thankfulness that she had been permitted to become an important instrument in the deliverance of her country, of honest pride at enjoying the esteem and gratitude of the King, and of security with regard to the future, inasmuch as she relied upon the protection of that Providence which had hitherto shielded her, her kinsfolk and friends, and the hills and valleys which she loved.

The night had scarcely enveloped the neighbouring mountains in thick darkness—a moonless night of June had been purposely chosen for the assembly—ere Dunmail, finding that, save the watchful sentinels whom he had himself nominated for their respective posts, all had retired to rest, stole forth from his palace in the infant city of Carlisle to see that his plans were efficiently carried into execution. He walked warily towards the earthen ramparts near which his intended victim had been lodged, when suddenly a light, like that from a burning censor, streamed upon his face, and for a moment dazzled his vision, when recovering himself, and looking up, he perceived that he was confronted by a stranger, attired like one of his own guards. He instantly accosted the stranger with the watchword which had been communicated to those only admitted to share his secret :—

"Dunmail?"

"Guonoline," was the ready reply, and the King, satisfied that there was no cause for apprehension, notwithstanding that the person of the soldier was unknown to him, was about to pass on, when the figure more authoritatively interposed :—

"Stay King," it said, in tones which betokened a habit of command, "I have sought for thee, and must now be heard."

"Thy name?" asked Dunmail.

"My business," answered the soldier, "concerns thy crown, thy kingdom, and thy life. The treacherous purpose for which thy selected guards are arrayed, and thou art here is known to me."

"And darest thou, hind, presume to interfere in what thy King has willed?"

"For thy sake, for the sake of Guonoline, whom thou would'st betray to infamy, and for the sake of Cumbria, the last faint hope of the ancient race of Britain, I would dare the vengeance of more powerful hands and subtler heads than thine."

The King put to his mouth a small whistle which depended from his baldrick, and blew a long, shrill blast which, piercing the heavy night air, returned in dull echoes upon the ear.

"It is vain to call for aid," resumed the soldier, "thy minions will not step between thee and me, and thou, perforce, shalt list to my mission."

There was that in the manner and accents of the stranger which filled Dunmail, King as he was, with a sense of fear and inferiority; and his arm being at the same moment gently seized, he followed without further question or resistance to a remote turret, which from its appearance might have been an abandoned watch-tower.

All that passed in this lonely chamber was never told: but it was whispered in after years—one knows not how such whispers get into circulation, revealing as they often do the most secret thoughts and acts of men, such as one never would voluntarily have entrusted to human being—that the King was there reminded of the night when he had sat abandoned and desolate amid the Druid circle on Potter-fell, of the promises he had then made to the fair vision which appeared to him, of his restoration to the throne from which he had been driven, and of the pledge—his life—with which he had bound his vow to follow the counsels of his deliverer, when his country should resume its independence. The King still hesitating as though in doubt, the stranger returned to him the golden amulet which had been taken from his neck for a sign of his acquiescence ; and demanded a final and irrevocable answer to the conditions which had been offered for his acceptance.

" Ask—demand anything, but the surrender of Guonoline," said Dunmail. " Why should my kingdom's peace or people's happiness be staked upon the thwarting of every hope or wish that is dear to me?"

" He that administers the law must himself be clear from the crimes which justice requires him to condemn and punish. This passion must be curbed and cured ; and Guonolino be left at freedom and in purity. Speak King; it is no idle sacrifice that is required from thee."

" I cannot subdue in my heart the love that the maiden has inspired."

" It will not warm thee in the grave," said the stern soldier.

" Nor will the passions which have agonised and maddened me on earth, swell there within my veins," replied the King.

" You refuse, then."

" Give me but a day for reflection."

" Thou hast had months of meditation, and ere another dawn thy foul purposes would be accomplished. Besides other considerations urge for resolve. Decide at once."

" I cannot relinquish the idol which I have so long worshipped."

" Enough ! The token of sovereignty upon thy finger—the talisman of thy success—is broken and destroyed, and the throne of Cumbria has departed from the lineage of King Dunmail."

Scarcely had this denunciation been uttered ere a shout as from the whole multitude then lodged within the palace or fortified station of Carlisle, arose upon the air, and the sound of armed men hurrying hither and thither, bearing torches and talking in brief and broken sentences, came indistinctly and like the echoes of a distant crowd, to murmur through the broken walls. Dunmail was terror-stricken, and, straining his eye-balls to penetrate the gloom, now rendered more palpable around the ruined tower by the flickering of

small lights, he sought the occasion of the unexpected
tumult. There was nothing, however, to indicate what
had befallen. He turned for an explanation to his
recent monitor; but the stranger had disappeared
without noise or sign, and left no trace or note of his
having been ever present, save on the memory of the
bewildered King. The latter stood aghast with horror
and despair for a moment, then rushing forth, soon
ascertained that a messenger had just brought in in_
telligence of a new descent of the Saxons, who had
captured and sacked the town of Kendal, and were
preparing again to overrun the kingdom. The monarch had been sought in every direction, and, being
found, a hasty council was summoned to devise measures to meet the emergency; but the wassail of the
evening was no fit induction to the midnight debate.
Ill-concerted plans were adopted—a gathering of the
clans of Cumbria was ordered; and the King disposed
his scarcely willing forces once more to meet the foe.

It would be idle to do more than trace the course of
events which ended in the overthrow of the last of the
British Kingdoms. Dunmail, his mind distracted by
the vision which had warned him of his coming doom,
was totally unfitted for the crisis; yet feeling that,
though he might fall in the conflict, his people's freedom might be secured, he made such hasty arrangements as he could for vigorous exertion, and advanced
across the moors and through the mountain defiles of
Cumberland, to offer battle to the host of Edmund.
Near the foot of Helvellyn, however, a spot where the
mountain rises abruptly, rent as it were from the
neighbouring hills by some long-forgotten convulsion
of nature, and a narrow pass is formed by the severed
rocks, his followers were surprised by a sudden onset
of the foe, who having been better informed of his

movements than he of theirs, had planted an ambuscade upon the jutting crags, among the ravines and dells, and on the wood-crowned acclivities around, and now descended like a torrent, freed from the obstruction of a winter's frost, to overwhelm and destroy him. The battle was stern and sanguinary, but it was brief. The King, who lacked neither the pride nor the courage of a hero, fell in the midst of his warriors, sword in hand, and rout and carnage were scattered far and wide through the beautiful pastoral valleys and dales of Westmorland and Cumberland. From end to end the Kingdom was pillaged and despoiled; and when it could yield no more to the ruthless victors, Edmund, the Saxon Monarch, bestowed the crown as a token of amity and a pledge of peace upon his friend and kinsman, Malcolm, King of Scotland.

Dunmail himself, and the flower of his chivalry, were buried where they fell, and a huge cairn or heap of stones was raised to honour their manes by the peasants of the surrounding district, who still loved their memory as the last link in the chain of British freedom. This tumulus still exists; and the herdsmen of the neighbourhood, in whose minds tradition has consecrated the great battle that gave their land to the Saxon, relate, in the long dark evenings of winter, round their cottage firesides, the unhappy love and disastrous end of this misguided Monarch; and sometimes when the wind rages among the rocky hills, and the blinding sleet drives along the ground, it is said that the phantom of the King may yet be seen pursuing a beautiful maiden, arrayed in white, who ever and anon seems placed within his grasp, but who, as he stretches his hand to seize her, vanishes in a snow wreath.

The fate of Guonoline is involved in obscurity.

v

When the shout arose which announced to the King at Carlisle that his foes had entered his dominion, a stranger—vested like a Druidess—entered her sleeping chamber, and apprizing her of impending danger which demanded instant flight, led her forth, and, placing her on a fleet horse, bade her speed towards the Scottish border. It is believed that she afterwards became the wife of a Celtic Chief beyond the Tweed, and that her descendants still exist among the noblest of the British peerage,—but this our legend saith not for certain.

The deeds and end of the true-hearted Leolf deserve a record of their own.

LEOLF, THE AVENGER.

[At the close of the Legend entitled *Dunmail Raise*, it was said, " The deeds and end of the true-hearted Leolf deserve a record of their own." The following brief narrative completes the story of that faithful friend and adherent of the "last King of Rocky Cumberland."]

When Dunmail perished at the foot of Helvellyn, he left two sons, Leoline and Hoel, both lads of tender age—too young to renew the struggle which had ended in their father's fall, but still old enough to give uneasiness to the victor, and to form rallying points to such of the conquered Cumbrians as might disdain to bow to the Saxon yoke. These princes it was the first care of Leolf, when he saw that the fortunes of his monarch on the field were irretrievable, to bear away to a place of concealment among the mountains; hoping to be enabled, ere long, to escape with them to the friendly borders of Strathclyde, whence, on some future opportunity, they might emerge to claim the crown and kingdom which the fate of war had now wrested from their grasp.

The Castle of Pendragon, however—remote, secluded, and strong as it was—was no place of security against

the minions of the remorseless Edmund, who, stealthily
tracing the vale of Eden with his iron-clad Saxons,
came upon the fortress before its inmates were prepared
for effective resistance, and capturing the sons of Dunmail, put out their eyes in sheer wantonness, and
retained them in his court among his buffoons and
minstrels, to minister to his pleasures. The cup of
affliction which had been forced upon the Britons was
full. Some of the inhabitants fled to the fastnesses of
Wales; others sought refuge in Scotland; a few found
means to pass over into Ireland and to Britany, and a
remnant accepted the grace of their Saxon lords, and
became serfs of the soil in the beautiful valleys which
beforetime they had cultivated as freemen and pro-
prietors.

Leolf, the royal cupbearer, put on the garb of a Saxon,
entered into the service of King Edmund, and watched
for the moment when, by one stroke, he might avenge
his sovereign, his princes and his country. Day by
day he wrought in secret to injure the oppressors of
his land. Was there a Saxon who needed aid, Leolf
would remove from him even the possibility of assistance. If disaffection crept into his household, and
among his bond-vassals, Leolf would foment the hatred
and fury of the conflicting parties, until violence and
bloodshed should ensue. The lawless he directed to
the homesteads of the wealthy, that their pride might
be humbled, and their joy dashed from their lips. He
covertly leagued himself with the daring and desperate,
both of his own countrymen and of the Danish and
Saxon people, whom discontent or crime urged to defy
the laws, or to seek the destruction of the King and
his race. And at last, on being detected as the accom-
plice of some daring freebooters, who sought to secure
the person of the King as he was journeying from Car-

lisle through the forest of Inglewood, he was driven to the woods, and forced to embrace for himself the life of an outlaw.

He now formed around him a band of armed Britons, which, increasing from day to day in numbers and prowess, soon spread terror and dismay around the country. The Saxons were nowhere secure but in their fastnesses. Their cattle were driven away, their vassals decoyed from their service, their houses and granaries fired in the dead of night, and even their castles stormed and sacked in the broad glare of the sun-light.

The King, who had returned to the South to exhibit the Trophies of his northern conquest before the eyes of the burghers of London, on hearing of the exploits of Leolf and his companions, was seized with rage and frenzy, and swore never to rest till he had extirpated the unconquerable Cumbrian race. He speedily gathered his forces; and about the middle of April hastened northwards to put his threats in execution—promulgating his *heriban* in every town and district through which he marched, in order to augment his power, by calling to his standard all the chiefs and people who owed him fealty and service, that by their aid his vengeance might be more signal and complete.

In those early times, however, a journey to the North was not accomplished so speedily as it is in these days. There were no roads save those which the Romans had left on their withdrawal from Briton ; and delays took place at every stage in the collection of food and forage : so that it was not till near the end of May that Edmund "the Magnificent" had reached the centre of his dominions.

At a small town on the borders of Staffordshire he halted on the feast of St. Augustine—the 26th of May —to commemorate the introduction of Christianity

among the Anglo-Saxons. Wassail filled his camp on
the occasion, and debauchery, for which the Saxons
were notorious among nations, and in which the sensual
clergy of the period mingled with a zest not inferior to
that of the soldiery, constituted the chief source of enjoyment to all. Minstrelsy and rude jesting filled the
intervals of what was intended for, and considerd a
solemn festival; and an almost universal licence prevailed among the rugged warriors and retainers, who
thronged the town.

The King, inflated with the pride of his pomp and
power, sat upon the throne, which formed part of his
baggage in all his expeditions, with one of the sons of
Dunmail lying on the rushes at his feet, and forming
his regal footstool. The other youth—Prince Leoline
—had sunk beneath the tyranny of his task-masters,
and left his history a blank. It was a strange, wild
scene—magnificently rude and incomprehensible as the
spirit-peopled halls of Valhalla, wherein the pirate sea-
kings and their followers—notwithstanding the mission
and preaching of the good Augustine, were still believed, by their semi-barbarous descendants, to hold
high carousals, and to drink strong ale and mead from
the skulls of their vanquished foes.

Suddenly a stranger minstrel arose in the midst of
the royal assembly, and touching the small rustic harp
which was slung from his shoulder, swept the strings
and drew forth a prelude of surpassing tenderness and
harmony. The mirth and revelry were hushed. The
jest died on the lips of the buffoon; the wine-cups and
ale-horns, were replaced upon the rough oaken tables,
and all eyes were at once turned upon the musician,
who thus commenced his measured but unrhymed
lay :—

"I had a dream—a dream of another world. I sat

at summer's dawn, in the hall where Odin reigns, and saw his chiefs preparing for the reception of those who should be slain in battle.

"I aroused the heroes with the tones of my harp, and bade them arrange the benches, and prepare the drinking cups for the reception of a king of their own lineage.

"' Whence comes he ?' exclaimed Woden. ' From the Isle of the slaughtered Britons,' I replied. ' 'Tis for Edmund, the proud, the magnificent. Arise, warriors, and go forth to meet and welcome him.'

"' And why,' asked Odin, the powerful, ' should the coming of King Edmund give joy to the dwellers in the land of spirits ?' ' Know ye not,' I exclaimed, ' that he hath stained his sword with blood—with the blood of babes and of women—that the grey hairs of the aged still cling to the heft of his *seax*, and bear testimony to his valour.'

"' Hail to thee—hail to thee, Edmund !' shouted the pirate wraiths aloud. ' Enter, brave warrior, among the host who wear kingly crowns !' "

A murmur ran through the crowd, swelling louder and louder as the minstrel proceeded ; and ere he had well concluded his strain, a hundred dirks were gleaming over the table—a hundred angry voices were raised to drown the treasonable song. The King started from his throne inflamed with rage and maddened with wine. He snatched a sword from the thane who sat nearest him, and rushed towards the undaunted minstrel, when his foot-bearer, prince Hoel, springing up, exclaimed in terror, "Touch him not, I conjure you, King ! 'Tis Leolf, my guardian !"

"Leolf—the outlaw !" was instantly echoed through the hall, and borne onward with shouts through the gathering crowd without.

"Aye, Leolf the Avenger!" coolly responded the undaunted minstrel; "come to demand atonement for the blood of his murdered sovereign and kinsmen."

The chiefs and warriors retreated a few paces from before the bold and resolute Cumbrian, whose prowess had come to be celebrated through the entire length and breadth of the kingdom.

"Seize him, and bear him to an instant death of torture," cried Edmund, his eye-balls swollen, and his lips quivering with fury.

A Saxon earl advanced to execute the command; but he was felled with a single blow of the Briton's clenched hand, and lay sprawling in agony among the rushes which covered the floor of earth. None other ventured to brave the wrath of the "robber"—as Leolf was called.

The King himself rushed forward to secure the intruder, and seizing him by his long hair, endeavoured to dash him to the ground. Leolf, however, had more muscular strength and more skill in wrestling than the King; and Edmund, instead of the outlaw, was overthrown in the struggle. No one sought to interpose; for surprise and awe had stricken all the beholders with a kind of stupor; and, ere they could recover from their surprise, Leolf had drawn forth a dagger— previously concealed in the folds of his plaid—and plunged it, with a loud exulting cry, into the monarch's heart. A yell of execration arose from the Saxon throng; and a moment afterwards, Leolf lay stretched beside his foe, pierced with a hundred wounds from the weapons of the guards and courtiers in the midst of whom his vengeance had been executed. His end, however, was accomplished. Edmund, in the flower of his age, and the spring-tide of his power and ambition, had been brought to the grave, and the Avenger could die content with the re- flection that he had saved his country from the desolation with which it had been threatened; know- ing, as he did, that from the wrath of the imbecile Edred, who was destined to succeed his brother on the Saxon throne, less was to be feared by his enemies than by his friends.

Concerning the fate of Prince Hoel, both history and tradition alike are silent.

LEE AND BELL, PRINTERS, FINKLE-STREET, KENDAL.

www.ingramcontent.com/pod-product-compliance
Lightning Source LLC
Chambersburg PA
CBHW022358020726
47500CB00002B/338